THE TIDE OF THE MERMAID TEARS

MARCIA LYNN McCLURE

Published by Distractions Ink
1290 Mirador Loop N.E.
Rio Rancho, NM 87144

©Copyright 2010, 2011, 2014 by M. L. Meyers
A.K.A. Marcia Lynn McClure
Cover Photography by ©Horst Kanzek/Dreamstime.com
and ©Willyvend/Dreamstime.com
Cover Design and Interior Graphics by Sandy Ann Allred/Timeless Allure

First Printed Edition: 2011
Second Printed Edition: 2014

McClure, Marcia Lynn, 1965—
The Tide of the Mermaid Tears: a novella/by Marcia Lynn McClure.

ISBN 978-0-9913878-4-7

Library of Congress Control Number: 2014943227

Printed in the United States of America

For Whimsical Inspiration…
And because I love Madonna's "Cherish" Video!

CHAPTER ONE
THE TIDE OF THE MERMAID TEARS

Ember walked. Rather, she meandered along the breadth of beloved seaside. So familiar was each large rock and expanse of sand along the shore, she fancied she could wander the margin blindfolded and still know her way. Quickly, however, she determined she would rather close her eyes in proving the adored familiarity of the course than be blindfolded, lest she miss some delicate sea treasure for the sake of the length of cloth necessary to mask her vision. She mused that were her eyes merely closed as she wandered, she could open them quickly and search the soft sand for pretty shells, ancient driftwood, and other trinkets the great Roman, Neptune, might scatter in her path. No. A blindfold would not allow treasure hunting. Therefore, Ember determined she could walk the seaside with her eyes closed instead.

Her morning treasure walks were one of Ember Taffee's greatest delights. Always there were familiar things to see and feel. The morning air was spiced with the rich scents of the water and the breeze, ocean foliage, and creatures of the sea. Ember inhaled a deep breath and smiled as the brisk zest of the sea air refreshed her senses. The breeze toyed with a strand of her acorn-colored hair, tickling her cheek and coaxing a giggle from her throat.

"My, you are playful this morning," she said aloud to the breeze. "It must be you sense a good day is upon us."

Yes, always there were things to see and feel along the shore near the cottage. Likewise, there were ever treasures to find. Ember woke each morning with a certain delight—an excited measure of eagerness in anticipating her daily meanders—for Ember Taffee was nothing if not a treasure hunter. To Ember, the seaside was a marvel of wealth, a treasure trove to be explored twice daily. Each morning she would rush to the shore to see what treasures and delights Neptune had strewn along her favored path. Each evening she would wander the breadth of the margin of shore near the cottage again, trolling for sea treasure. Low tide was preferable for treasure hunting, of course. But even when the tide was in, there was booty to be found. Whether it was a branch of worn driftwood, a pretty shell, or some such other treasure, Ember delighted in finding Neptune's discarded trinkets as fully as any pirate delighted in hoarding a chest of doubloons. Already she'd found three pretty shells on her morning meander along the shore that day—a pretty rose-petal tellin shell, one nutmeg shell, and one half of a set of angel wings. The angel wing was her favorite, of course, being rare and very large— near to five inches long, she surmised. Oh, how she wished to find a complete set of angel wings one day. In her quiet thoughts, she referred to it as her "shell dream"—a secret hope of finding a set of both the pretty clamshells that had managed to remain together somehow.

The sun had risen long ago. Ember knew her mother would be anxious for her return, and her sister, Lily, would be awake, no doubt—awake and complaining over the tasks needing to be done. Ember knew she should not tarry long. Still, she could not abandon the shore yet. She sensed there was more—more than merely the three pretty shells in her apron pocket.

Three gulls swooped to the water's surface. Ember shaded her eyes and watched them—listened to their gull-calls as they frolicked in the sun and surf. The sun was bright and stung her eyes, and she glanced down a moment to cool them.

Instantly, a smile spread across her face, a thrill of glee and enchantment traveling through her every limb. There, in the sand just near the toe of her right boot, she saw it—a mermaid tear!

"Oh, let pirates have their golden booty!" she giggled. "But leave me nature's jewels!"

Quickly, she bent and retrieved the small, smooth piece of glass from the sand. Far smaller than a penny, the water-worn piece of amber glass was as beautiful to Ember's dark brown eyes as any ruby or emerald.

"A mermaid tear," she whispered, turning the glass sea jewel over and over in her hand.

Ember squealed with delight, clutched the tiny mermaid tear to her bosom, and looked to the sand about her feet. Oh, it was well she knew that sea glass was rare. To find one was a blessing. No one knew how long it took the sea to smooth the sharp edges of pieces of broken bottles into mermaid tears—years, at least. Thus, each small piece of sea glass—each mermaid tear—was indeed a treasure, and one should not hope to find more. Yet Ember did hope—as ever she did.

She gasped, a second squeal of delight erupting from her throat as she bent to retrieve a cobalt-blue bottle top. Ember giggled as she studied the broken top, smooth and now milky, of what was once most likely a poison bottle, for it was poison that was most often stored in bottles of cobalt blue. It was small and lovely—well worn—and she wondered how it had found its way to the sea.

Ember looked again and dropped to her knees in the sand. She smiled, thrilled as she found three more pieces of amber sea glass nearby. She held five in all—five tears of a mermaid.

"Did you love a sailor?" Ember asked aloud. "Did you follow his ship? Was he lost and you wept for your love?" Then she remembered the full moon of the night before. Legend said mermaids could only come ashore during the full moon—that pieces of sea glass were their tears changed to glass as they dripped to the sand when the mermaids left at dawn to return to the sea.

"Or were you simply sad to leave us as the sun rose?" she whispered, studying the pieces of sea glass once more. "I am sorry for your pain," Ember said, glancing out to the waves of the sea. "But I thank you for leaving your tears for me to find."

Oh, Ember did not believe in mermaids—not anymore. She was far too grown up to believe in fairy tales and myths. Still, she liked to pretend she still believed in them—liked to imagine beautiful mermaids frolicking among the waves of the sea, watching over the sailors they loved from afar, venturing onto the shore by the light of the full moon. And so she often spoke to the sea, imagining the mermaids and others of Neptune's realm were truly listening.

Once more she studied the sand beneath her feet. Oh, Ember well knew five mermaid tears were more than she could ever have hoped to find on one seaside morning. Yet a true treasure seeker was always hopeful—never forced the eye from the space that might cache hidden riches. Thus, she lingered a few moments longer in hopeful searching.

At last, however, she sighed. Five mermaid tears were all the mermaids had left for her that morning, and she was profoundly glad for them.

Carefully, she dropped them in her apron pocket—a different pocket than the one protecting the pretty shells. She closed her eyes a moment, inhaled the salty sea air, and walked forward. One step, then two—her eyes still closed. She could hear the gulls above the surf, hear the water lapping against the rocks just out beyond the sandy shore.

She took two more steps and paused—squeezed her eyes tightly shut and listened. The gulls—the water—yet there was something else. She listened harder, concentrating on the unfamiliar sound.

Instantly, her eyes popped open as she half expected to see a lingering mermaid on the sand, gasping for breath. Gasping—coughing! That was the unfamiliar sound.

Ember gasped herself as she looked forward, up the shore, to see a man struggling in the water. He was coughing and spitting water from his mouth as he crawled from the water and onto the sand. As he collapsed facedown on the shore, Ember lifted her skirt and ran toward him.

Her mother's voice echoed in her mind, warning her to be guarded. *Use your heart to distinguish that of another,* she heard her mother's voice caution in her head.

Ember paused a moment, inhaling a deep, calming breath. There was a man lying on the beach—a strange man. Was he to be trusted? Calling on the same gift her mother owned—the gift of determining a soul—Ember waited for an answer to her silent question.

The answer did not take long to come. As her heart swelled with assurance that all would be well, she again ran toward the man, dropping to her knees beside him.

"Sir?" she cried, nudging one broad shoulder. The man was stripped of his shirt, dressed only in a pair of trousers, no shoes. Ember's imaginative fancy briefly wondered if mermaids really did exist—or rather, mermen. Perhaps the man was one of Neptune's children who had lingered too long during the full moon and would now die for having failed to return to the sea before dawn. Ember shook her head, rolling her eyes at her own foolishness.

"Sir?" she called again, nudging his broad shoulder once more. The man lay on his stomach, his face turned away from her. "Are you dead, sir?" she asked. Placing a hand to his back, she sighed with relief as she felt he yet breathed.

"Sir?" she said, clambering over the man's broad back. "Sir, are you...?" Ember gasped as she looked to the man's face, half buried in the sand. Again she wondered at the existence of mermen, for surely no human man could be so handsome. He was dark-haired, with a strong, straight nose and a squared, rather chiseled-looking jaw.

The man coughed. His eyes opened—his deep blue eyes, so shaded by thick, wet lashes that Ember wondered how it was he could see beyond them.

"Sir?" Ember ventured.

He coughed, asking, "Where am I?"

"On the seashore, sir," Ember answered.

The man coughed again—slightly grinned. Ember fancied a quiet chuckle accompanied his coughing.

"The seashore, you say, girl?" he asked, still coughing.

"Yes, sir," Ember answered.

Ember looked to the sea. She saw no ship—no wreckage to mark that a ship had run arock. She saw no evidence of a boat of any sort.

"How came you to be here, sir?" she asked. "Were you wrecked? There are wreckers that haunt these shores at times…though I have not heard of any of late. Were you, indeed, wrecked, sir?"

"No," he mumbled. He coughed again, and Ember began to push at his shoulder—an effort to roll him over to his back. "Oh! You are a brute, aren't you?" she mumbled as she pushed at him. "Please…sit up. Is there water in your lungs, do you think?"

He coughed and struggled to turn and push himself to a sitting position. "No," he said, yet spitting water from his mouth. "I don't think so."

Still, for all his assurances, Ember worried. "Here," she said, placing the side of her face to his broad chest. "Let me listen." She closed her eyes, trying to listen—trying to discern any rattle in his lungs. But the sea was too near—too loud—and she could hear nothing in him save the rhythmic beating of a strong heart.

"Come along," she said, tugging at one of his large hands as she struggled to her feet. "We must get you home. My mother must give you a thorough going-over." She heaved on his arm, but he was so large—far too heavy for her small frame to dominate. "Sir, you must come with me," she ordered. "You are far too chilled! We must warm you and determine your state."

"My state is that of wellness, I assure you," he said, finally rising to his feet.

Yet as he stumbled forward, nearly knocking Ember to the ground with his massive weight, she shook her head, scolding, "You are not well. How long have you been in the sea?"

"Hours," he admitted.

"Come then," she ordered. "Mother must see to you at once."

"But I am a stranger, miss," the man told her as she draped one of his massively muscular arms across her own shoulders.

"Yes," she admitted. "But you are obviously in no condition to molest me in any manner. Therefore, I must see to your welfare."

She heard him chuckle—thought it odd the man should be so mirthful, considering his circumstances.

"I am glad to see you find humor in your situation, sir," she told him, "though I certainly would not be so entertained were I in your shoes."

"I'm not wearing any shoes," the man said.

Ember smiled. How jovial he was! She liked him at once for his sense of humor in the face of obvious tribulation.

He stumbled, nearly taking himself and Ember to the sand.

"Careful," she warned. "If you crush me to death, we'll never make it to the cottage."

His arm was heavy about her shoulders. Ember felt as if she were a tiny pony laden with a monstrous burden to carry. He stumbled again, and a quick shriek of surprise escaped Ember's throat as she tumbled to the ground, the stranger's massive body crushing hers into the sand.

"Forgive me," he said, weakly lifting his body from atop hers, struggling to his feet. She thought it very gallant that he then offered her his hand as assistance. The man could hardly stand, yet he was enough of a gentleman to offer to help her. She accepted his hand and was somewhat surprised at the power in his arm allowing him to pull her to standing before him once more.

"Come along," she said, taking his hand. "We are very near the cottage." She turned, leading him toward her home. He stumbled twice more, collapsing to his knees once. Still, he stood and trudged onward.

"What's your name, miss?" the stranger asked.

"Ember," Ember answered. "Ember Taffee. And yours?"

"Ridge W-Westm…Ridge West," he stammered.

"Well, Ridge West," Ember began as they climbed the small hill above the shore to see her family's cottage a short distance off, "welcome to Trident Point and Taffee Cottage."

Ridge said nothing. Trident Point? Taffee Cottage? His mind still swam from swimming; his body yet ached with the exertion of his ordeal. From Bay Warwick to Trident Point? Is that all the farther the ship had sailed before he'd been forced to jump overboard?

He shook his head, too tired and worn to consider the events that now found him following a pretty young woman to her family home. He smiled, realizing how truly exhausted he must be, for he'd thought certain he dreamt her at first. When he'd opened his eyes to see this Ember Taffee kneeling next to him—the sea breeze toying with her long, soft hair, the dark, near black of her eyes peering into his own—he'd thought surely he'd been lost to madness, that she was an angel sent to collect his soul. Yet she held his hand; he could feel her touch, feel the ache of his legs and arms as he struggled to follow her. The fatigue and pain in him were proof he was indeed still living. Somehow he'd managed to make the swim to shore, and as he glanced up to the cottage before him, he mused he'd never seen a more welcoming sight in all his life.

The cottage was small and inviting in appearance. Many windowed and clean whitewashed, it seemed to beckon him—bid him enter the cozy walls. Its windows gleamed in the morning sun, and he thought he'd never seen so many plants thriving in so many colors so near to the sea.

"Mother!" his rescuer called, tugging even more determinedly on his hand. "Mother! Come quickly!"

Ridge growled as his knees buckled. He collapsed upon them in the grassy margin before the cottage. His head was spinning, his body beginning to shiver uncontrollably.

"Mother! Quickly!" the girl cried, dropping to her knees before him.

He thought how warm her palms were as she took his face in her hands—searched his eyes almost pleadingly.

"The shivers are overtaking you," she told him. He felt her thumbs travel over his lips as his vision blurred. "You must be warmed. I cannot carry you, sir!" she pleaded. "I cannot—you are three of me! You must rise and walk the rest of the way. Look…just there," she said, nodding her head to indicate the cottage. "Just inside there is warmth and rest. Come with me."

Ridge shook his head and bit his tongue hard in an effort to regain his full wits.

"Ember!" a woman's voice called. "What is it?"

Ridge glanced up as another lovely, free-haired woman approached. This one was older than his rescuer. He assumed this was the mother she had spoken of. Her hair was the same color as her daughter's, only her eyes were two green emeralds instead of the mysterious dark pools of her daughter's.

"Lily! Help us!" Ember cried as another young woman appeared. This young woman was beautiful as well, owning her mother's emerald eyes, with hair as black as obsidian loosely braided and hanging over one shoulder.

"Who is he?" the eldest woman inquired.

"Ridge West," Ember told her. "I found him on the shore. He is very weak."

"Let's get him inside," Ember's mother said. "He must be stripped and warmed at once. Help us, Lily."

Ridge shook his head and tried to rally his senses. But he was dizzy, weak, and unable to walk of his own accord.

As the three women struggled to manage him into the cottage, he cursed himself for such weakness. The trembling for the cold his body was experiencing was overwhelming; his teeth ached from being so tightly clenched.

It seemed mere moments, and he was within the warm walls of the small cottage. A fire burned in a nearby hearth, and it was there before it that the three women deposited him. He had no strength to raise himself and determined that the soft rug beneath him was the warmest, most comfortable surface he would ever know.

"Lily," the matron began, "rummage through the old trunk. See if you can find something of your father's that might fit this man."

"Yes, Mother," the one called Lily said.

"Loose his trousers. We must strip him, dry him, and see that he begins to warm," the matron said to the girl who had found him.

"No!" he growled, pushing the girl's hands from his waist as she began to obey her mother's instruction.

"You must be warmed," the eldest women said, taking his chin firmly in hand and forcing his attention to her face. "Ember, his trousers," she said over her shoulder.

"She's only a girl, madam," Ridge mumbled. His need to remain a gentleman—even under such threatening circumstances to his well-being—was thoroughgoing through him. He would not have the whole of his form displayed before her innocent eyes.

The mother of his rescuer smiled. "She is full nineteen, sir," she said. "But I will see that her innocence remains unscathed. You are heroic to be concerned for her."

Ridge shook his head and mumbled, "I am no hero, madam."

He felt the woman place a blanket over him at his waist.

"I will strip him, Ember," the woman said. "You begin warming him. Chafe his chest and then his shoulders, arms, and hands."

Ridge breathed relieved as the daughter leaned over him then.

"You are fortunate that I lingered on my morning walk, sir," Ember told him, smiling.

"Y-yes," he said between chattering teeth.

With trembling hands, he reached beneath the blanket the girl's mother had spread over him and, using the last ounce of strength in him, pushed his trousers and undergarments to his knees. After all, he knew the wisdom of the matron; he might die if he did not warm his body soon. He sighed as he felt the eldest woman strip his trousers and undergarments completely from him and tuck the blanket securely around his hips and upper thighs, ensuring a shred of modesty at least.

Ember's palms were warm on the cooled flesh of his chest. She paused, combing small fingers through his wet hair and pushing at his cheek so that his head turned, allowing his face to feel the warmth of the fire.

"Mother, I doubt Father's trousers will fit him in length in the least," the one called Lily said, returning at that moment.

"They will do for now. See to his arms, Lily," the matron whispered.

He felt his legs being chafed—his arms—his shoulders. He chuckled slightly, thinking he had chums that had paid wages to less genteel ladies in seeking such treatment.

"He is either mad or in possession of a rare sense of humor," he heard his rescuer tell her mother. This only caused him to chuckle again, however.

"Let us hope it is simply amusement and not madness then," the sister, Lily, said.

"He is yet in danger, my darlings," the mother said. "We will need to tend him thoroughly and well if we are to preserve him."

Ridge could feel warmth then—the tiniest breath of warmth. It began in the center of his chest, and he sensed it would spread. As Ember's small, soft hands kneaded the flesh of his torso, Ridge's eyes closed at last. Weariness was sore over him, and he could barely rein in consciousness.

"I do wonder how it is you always happen upon the most unexpected things, Ember," he heard the sister say. "Is he dangerous, Mother?"

Ridge desired respite more than anything. Yet he would hear the matron's answer first—before he rested.

"No," came the answer. "He will not do us any bodily harm."

How the matron came by her judgment, he knew not. Still, he was pleased in her correct assessment of him.

"Chafe him with more exuberance, Lily!" he heard Ember scold. "Neptune did not let me find him in order that he may die here in our care!"

"He is not a shell or a bit of sea glass you have collected, Ember!" Lily snapped. "You cannot keep him in a bottle on the mantel!"

"That would depend upon the size of the bottle," Ember retorted.

Ridge smiled—breathed one final chuckle as the darkness of restful oblivion laid claim to him.

"He sleeps," Tempest Taffee whispered to her daughters. "We must chafe him awhile longer. Then we will leave him to his rest."

"Where did he come from?" Lily asked. She was frowning when she looked to Ember.

Ember merely shrugged. "From the sea," she answered plainly—for it was the only truth she knew.

Lily rolled her eyes with exasperation, but Ember knew not what else to answer.

"He is a fine figure of a man," Tempest said. "So strong, muscular, and healthy, save the danger he is in now." She shook her head. "This is no vagabond or skulking criminal."

"Look how handsome he is!" Lily breathed, running a hand over his powerful arm, studying the calluses on his palm. "No sailor was ever so handsome. Ouch!" Lily exclaimed as Ember slapped the back of her hand.

"He is not a shell or a bit of sea glass I have collected, Lily. You cannot keep him in a bottle on the mantel," Ember teased, using Lily's own mocking words.

"Chafe, darlings! Chafe…else the world may not keep him at all," Tempest told them.

"Yes, Mother," Ember said, renewing her efforts to warm the man's torso.

Ember gazed into the stranger's restful, mythically handsome face as she chafed his flesh. By far he was the most beautiful sea treasure Neptune had ever strewn in her path. She silently wished that the Roman god of the sea were real—that he had truly intended to send her a man so beautiful as to warm her heart. In the next thought, however, Ember scolded herself for her childish musings, for of two things she was most certain: there was no Neptune, god of the sea, and a warm heart only brought pain to she who bore it.

Chapter Two
A SON OF NEPTUNE

Ember sat on the soft rug before the hearth fire—sat knees drawn up, arms encircling them. She remained still, warm, and serene—and entirely intrigued! Surely she'd never seen such a handsome man— such a broad-shouldered, muscular man—not in all her life! Even living near the shore, where fishermen and sailors frequented the town and surrounding areas, often wearing naught but their trousers and shoes. No, Ember Taffee had never seen such a man before.

The stranger called Ridge West moaned slightly in his sleep, grimaced, and turned his face toward her. Ember studied him longer still—his dark hair and the way it fell softly across his forehead. His eyes were closed in resting, it was true, shaded by sleep and long, dark lashes. Still, she would never forget their vibrant blue. His chin was strong and with an ever so slight cleft, his jaw square and in need of a shave. His nose was straight and neither small nor large. Ember watched, entranced as his broad chest rose and fell with his breathing.

Twilight was ebbing; the sun would soon dip beyond the sea, bringing night. Her mother and Lily had each taken turns in watching over the handsome castaway, and now it was again Ember's turn. Her mother had explained that he must be allowed to rest until wakefulness found him naturally. Thus, Ember sat near to him, listening to his rhythmic breathing, having written the events of the morning in her diary—for these were events to be recorded indeed! It was not every day that a girl found a man washed ashore—a man so handsome as to put her in mind of Neptune's legendary merfolk of the deep. Long ago, Ember's father had told her many tales of merfolk. They had been her favorite stories to hear as a small child—her favorite dreams to dream. She smiled, thinking that, had she found the stranger a decade earlier, she would certainly have thought him a wayward son of Neptune. Still, she knew it was best to simply write her thoughts and musings in her diary, and she had done so.

There was naught else to do now but wait—wait on the man, see if he would live or if the exertion of fighting in the sea would take him. She knew he would live, however. Such a man could not be bested by the mere power of the sea. She wished for just a moment that her heart was not so spoiled, so weary of men and their lack of feeling. Perhaps then, if the stranger from the sea did not prove to be already spoken for, she would've considered allowing him to touch her heart a little. Still, even for her young age, Ember Taffee knew men—knew their hearts did not beat so loving and loyal as a woman's.

He moved and shifted his position, and Ember gasped, covering her eyes, lest the blankets protecting his modesty should shift. She heard him settle and carefully peeked through her fingers. She sighed, for all was well. He still lay on his back, one arm resting at his side, the other forearm across his forehead.

"Has he wakened at all? Even a moment?" Lily asked in a whisper. Approaching from behind, Lily sat next to Ember, tucking her nightdress around her legs.

"No," Ember answered quietly.

"I'll sit with him through the night," Tempest offered in a whisper as she knelt beside the man—studied him a moment.

"No! Let me!" Ember exclaimed. "Please? I'll call you if he wakes. I cannot bear to abandon him."

"Abandon him?" Lily asked, frowning. "He's not a homeless kitten, Ember."

"Lily," Tempest soothed.

But Lily continued to frown. "She'll be wanting to put him on a chain and wear him round her neck next, Mother!"

"And wouldn't you like to wear such a man round your neck, darling?" Tempest teased her eldest daughter.

"Mother!" Lily exclaimed, scolding her mother, though she did smile at being bested in wits—and amused.

"I'm not certain it should be you who sits up with him, Ember," Tempest said.

"Oh, he'll not harm me if he wakes, Mother," Ember said. "He'll most likely sleep through all the night anyway. And I do feel somewhat...somewhat responsible for him."

"Oh, responsible, is it?" Lily teased. "Is that what you're feeling?"

"Mother," Ember pleaded, ignoring her sister's mockery.

Tempest studied the stranger for a long moment. Ember knew her mother was determining his soul once more—deciding whether it were safe to leave Ember alone with him.

As her mother looked back to her, Ember sighed. Her mother's eyes were soft, void of concern or trepidation. "You call for me the instant he wakes," Tempest said. "Better yet, come and wake me. Do you promise?"

"I do," Ember agreed.

"Very well," Tempest said, yawning. "I am more worn than a sea pebble." Again Tempest nodded to Ember, reminding, "Fetch me if he wakes, Ember."

"I will, Mother," Ember assured her.

"And don't do anything silly, Ember," Lily said, also yawning.

"Silly?" Ember asked. "Such as?"

"Oh, I don't know," Lily sighed. "Just don't do anything silly."

Ember exchanged cheek-kisses with her mother and Lily as well.

"Good night, my darling," Tempest said.

"Good night," Ember whispered.

"Remember, nothing silly," Lily teased, winking at her sister before following her mother out of the room.

Ember sighed, glad to be alone with her thoughts once more—glad to be alone with the stranger from the sea once more. Returning her attention to her silent pondering, she wondered where the man had come from. Was he a sailor? She thought not, for no sailor was ever built of such bulking muscle. Sailors were far too underfed to boast such forms as the man asleep before the hearth. A villain perhaps? No, her mother would not have determined his soul to be a safe one to enter the house then—nor would have Ember. Perhaps he was a stowaway.

Ember's musings ceased, however, for her eyelids were heavy and her mind tired—and her body. Pulling a blanket from the nearby sofa, she lay down on the floor near the stranger. She moved closer to him, that she might continue to hear him breathe—wake up if the rhythm of his breathing changed or stopped. Tucking her hands beneath her head, she gazed into his handsome face.

"It's unfortunate that a woman must guard her heart from the wiles of men," she whispered, "else you might have touched mine."

The fire burned warm, the stranger from the sea breathed soft, and Ember closed her eyes.

☼

Ridge drew a deep breath. The scents and sounds that met his first wakeful moments enveloped him in a cloud of comfort and tranquility. A clock—a steady, rhythmic ticking—enriched by the scent of lavender and mint, of wood burning, and of the faint yet lingering aroma of new bread.

He tried to open his eyes, but they were yet heavy. He was too warm—not overly warm, just too warm—the warmth that beckoned continued slumber. Still, he must awaken. Thus, he forced his eyes to open. He was lying on his back, a ceiling above him. It was unfamiliar. He glanced to his left. There was a hearth there—also unfamiliar—but very comforting and warm. Slowly he turned his head to his right, squeezing his eyes tightly for a moment and then forcing them wide in an effort to draw himself to better awareness.

He frowned when he saw that a young woman lay next to him. She was curled on her side, facing him, her small hands tucked prayerfully under her rosy cheek, a blanket covering her. He shook his head a little—rubbed at his eyes with one sore hand. He'd dreamt of such a young woman—dreamt that a strange beauty with windblown hair and eyes as dark as midnight had pulled him from the sea. He looked to the young woman once more. The only light in the room was the light from the dying embers in the hearth, and it made clear vision difficult. The fire—embers. He remembered then.

"Ember," he whispered.

Yet he was nearly certain he was still dreaming. Again he rubbed his eyes, resting his other hand on his chest—his bare chest. Instantly, full consciousness was his. He tugged at the blanket covering him from the waist down. He lifted it—frowned when he saw he was naked beneath.

Shaking his head again, which had begun to hammer with the pain of hunger and exertion, he glanced to the girl at his right and then back to himself and his lack of attire. He could not remember stripping himself. Anxiety began to rise in him at his inability to clearly remember the events that found him now thus. He lifted the blanket covering him once more to ensure he had not imagined he was not clothed. Disturbed, he looked to the young woman. Reaching out, he carefully lifted the blanket covering her, sighing with relief when he saw she was fully clothed. At least the sea had not driven his wits from him, causing him to behave wickedly.

He closed his eyes a moment, trying to remember, trying to calm himself. Yes. It came to him then. He'd jumped. It had been necessary to jump from the ship and into the sea. He remembered seeing the lighthouse. He'd managed to swim to a rock near shore and wait until the sun rose so that he could swim to the sand without risking tearing his body to shreds on more rocks. At last he'd crawled from the water, coughing and spitting, and been discovered by this young woman now at his side.

"Ember," he mumbled.

He remembered she'd assisted him to a cottage and remembered her mother and sister then—that they'd stripped and chafed him. It was all his weary mind could recall. How long he'd lain on the rug in front of the fire in the cottage he did not know. He surmised there was no man about, for no man would have allowed a stranger to linger before the fire. No husband, father, or brother would have set a young woman as sentinel over him.

He turned his head toward the pretty girl once more and gazed at her a long moment. Unexpectedly, her eyes opened, and she stared at him without moving. The dark irises of her eyes were enthralling—alluringly inviting. Ridge imagined for a moment that the soft midnight pools of her vision might somehow absorb his soul—or that the girl herself might possess the power to bewitch him, enslave him to her will.

"Are you wakeful…or am I dreaming?" she whispered.

"You're not dreaming," he answered—though he was not so fully sure that *he* was not dreaming. She smiled, and he felt the corners of his own mouth curve slightly in return.

He was astonished when she reached out, brushing his hair from his forehead and whispering, "I knew you would recover." She sat up then, still smiling. "You must be hungry," she said. "I'll fetch my mother."

He watched her disappear into the dark shadows of the cottage. He struggled to raise himself; every muscle, every bone ached as he'd never known muscle and bone could ache. He grimaced—grunted—but managed to sit up. He drew his legs up, resting his elbows on his knees and raking sore fingers through his tousled hair.

He yawned, feeling a great fatigue even yet. He glanced to the floor next to him to see a neatly folded pile of clothing. Mustering what strength he could, he pulled on the underdrawers and trousers, both of which were too tight to fit comfortably, the trousers being far too short in length. He cared not, however, and collapsed to his back once more, the exertion of the simple act of dressing himself far more taxing than it would normally have been.

"There you are," the matron said, entering the room. Her two daughters followed, and Ridge was glad he'd managed the trousers. "How are you feeling? Better?"

Ridge nodded and struggled to raise himself to sitting again. "Yes, milady," he said. "Much better…though admittedly not myself."

"Milady?" the woman giggled. "Oh, dear, no! You may call me Tempest."

Ridge nodded. "Very well," he agreed.

"Ember," Tempest began, looking to the girl who had found him, "fetch two of the eggs I boiled yesterday…and a slice of bread."

"Yes, Mother," Ember said. Ridge watched her disappear into another room.

"We'll feed you a little something, Ridge West," Tempest told him. "Then we'll hear your story and decide what must be done."

Ridge nodded. Humbly he said, "Thank you, ma'am. It was a valiant, albeit dangerous thing you did…taking a strange man in…caring for him."

Tempest pulled her shawl more snuggly about her shoulders as she smiled. "No doubt Neptune placed you on our shore for a reason, Mr. West," she said.

Ridge heard the one called Lily giggle.

"Indeed," she said. "Just you hope that my sister doesn't come across a bottle large enough to plop you into, Mr. West. Else you'll be a souvenir of the sea to set on our mantel too." The girl nodded, indicating the mantel above the hearth behind him.

Ridge turned and looked at the mantel. Bottle after bottle adorned it, each filled with shells, sea glass, starfish, or other such ocean treasures.

"It's a hearty mantel indeed," Ridge began. Looking back to Lily, however, he added, "Though I doubt it would bear my weight…or the bottle meant to keep me there."

Tempest and Lily both giggled, and Ridge thought it quite the nicest sound in the world—the laughter of tender women.

He watched as Lily glanced to the floor, as she bent and picked up a small book lying there. "I see she's been writing her fancies again," Lily muttered, opening the book and leafing through the pages of handwritten entries.

"I'll thank you to keep your thoughts as private as I prefer to keep mine," Ember said, returning with a plate of boiled eggs and bread and a large mug. Setting the plate and mug on the floor next to Ridge, she turned, snatching the book from her sister.

Immediately, Ridge lifted the mug, draining it of the cool, refreshing water within. He moved himself so that his back could rest against the leg of the small sofa.

"Eat the eggs first, darling," Tempest said.

He nodded and bit into one of the eggs.

Ember gracefully sat herself on the floor in front of him, Lily sliding down next to her. Tempest, however, took her seat on the sofa.

"Do you remember how you found yourself ashore, Mr. West?" Tempest asked.

Ridge paused, deciding how much truth to tell them. He would not lie—would not make up some travesty of adventure. Still, he knew he must guard a part of the truth—omit certain details—else he find himself somehow cornered once more.

Ember waited, watching as the man ate one of the eggs. He would be thirsty—she knew he would—for he'd drained the mug of water as if he hadn't had a drink in a month. Quickly she snatched the mug, racing to the kitchen and refilling it for him. She returned and set it on the floor next to his plate, settling herself beside Lily once more.

"Thank you," he said to her, his sea-blue eyes gazing at her a moment and causing her stomach to feel light.

"I do remember. I...um...I jumped ship," he said.

"But you don't look like a sailor," Lily observed aloud.

"I'm not," he said, "though I was working my way down the coast...on a ship...working for payment of passage aboard a merchant ship."

"And you jumped," Tempest said. "Why?"

"I will tell you what I am willing, ma'am," the man explained. "But I would beg you to understand that any more might place me in...in discomfort, to say the least."

"Very well," Tempest agreed. "Then tell us what you will."

He nodded. Ember watched him, noting his discomfort.

"I was working for a merchant in a northern port, but...but for reasons I cannot reveal...I was forced to leave that employ. I found work on a ship, a ship headed south along the coast. I planned to find another position with another merchant some distance from where I had last labored. However, some of the sailors on the ship discovered my...determined to keep me aboard the ship until...determined to use me to force cruelty and pain on another."

"How would keeping you aboard a ship force cruelty and pain on someone?" Ember asked.

"I can't explain that...rather I won't," Ridge answered. "Yet I will tell you that I would not be held against my will, used as a pawn in a political venue of any sort. Thus, when I saw the lighthouse last night as we passed, I jumped ship...swam to a large rock and waited 'til morning to swim to shore."

Ember felt the frown puckering her brow. She sighed, thinking she would have preferred him to lie—say he was Neptune's own son, washed up and made human as penance for some misdeed—rather than to give them so little information.

"I have entrusted you with this truth, milady," Ridge said, taking Tempest's hand. "Each of you," he added, looking to Ember and Lily. "For I owe you the debt of saving my life, and I vowed to be truthful...as truthful as I could without hurting others. And now I would beg you, good ladies—I would beg your allegiance in keeping my secret."

He paused a moment, rubbing his temples with one hand before saying, "If you will lend me the price of one telegram, Mrs. Taffee, I will work the sum off in whatever chores you need doing here. Then I will venture to the nearest town in search of employment." Ember watched as the man looked to her mother. "Will you lend me the price of one telegram, milady? I swear to you, I will return the price to you with an interest sum as soon as I am able, or by whatever work you set forth for me."

"Are you married then?" Lily asked. "Do you have a wife and children to notify of your being alive?"

The man shook his head. "No. But I must let...my friends know I am well."

Ember looked to her mother—watched as Tempest Taffee gazed into the man's bluest of blue eyes. She was determining his soul once more, though Ember knew the man was not aware of it. Few people knew of Tempest's gift of determining a soul—of Ember's like gift.

"I believe you are telling us the truth, Ridge West," Tempest said at last. Ember sighed and glanced to Lily to see her sister smiling with relief as well. "As soon as you are well and able," Tempest continued, "we will take you to town to send your telegram."

"Thank you, Mrs. Taffee," Ridge said.

Ember smiled, nearly giggling with delight as Ridge took her mother's hand then, placing a grateful kiss to the back of it. "You and your daughters…you are creatures of profound compassion."

Lily gasped as the man unexpectedly reached out and took hold of her hand. Ember was disturbed by the heat of jealousy that rose in her as she watched the man place his lips to Lily's hand in gratitude.

"Thank you, Miss Taffee," he told her. Ember watched Lily's face grow rosy with delight.

Silently she thought, *Surely he will kiss my hand as well. After all, I am she who found him.*

In the next moment, Ember felt a long-absent fluttering in her bosom as the man did, indeed, take her hand.

"And thank you…you, my rescuer," he said, pressing a soft kiss to the back of her hand. "I believe you saved my life," he added, turning her hand over and pressing a kiss into her palm.

As delighted as Ember was by his touch—as euphoric as his gesture caused her to feel—it likewise caused too much sensitivity in Ember. Uncomfortable with her own breathlessness, Ember gently pulled her hand from his grasp and said, "You're welcome, though it was you who jumped from the ship, endured a night in the sea, and swam to shore. I did not do that."

Ridge's eyes narrowed as he studied the girl. Her entire body had begun to quiver the moment he'd touched her. He'd felt her pulse increase as well, for his thumb had lingered over the place on her wrist just where her heartbeat was discernable. Yet suspicion rose in him, and he felt her quivering was borne more of sudden fear than for being pleased by his gratitude. He sensed that though Ember Taffee was strong, endowed with a playful nature and certain delight in life, there was something else—something masked and not in accordance with the happy nature she outwardly displayed.

He was distracted as Tempest giggled and said, "Well, it is certain you cannot traipse about in my husband's old clothes. It's a wonder you fastened the trousers. As soon as I am dressed, I will go to town and fetch some things more befitting your size."

"Oh, please, no," Ridge said. He was horrified at his forced humility—his certain dependence on three cottage women. "I cannot beg to burden you for the price of clothing…not until the telegram is sent and—"

"You will simply owe me a greater debt, Mr. West…prideful man that you are," Tempest said. "It is only that simple."

Ember watched as the stranger's jaw clenched. He was humiliated—she could see that he was.

"It is not my practice to be a burden to others," he rather growled, "whether the cost is intruding on a home…or where other means are concerned."

"It is why God gives us such trials as yours, Mr. West," Tempest began, "to remind us of our humility…and to allow others the opportunity to serve."

Ember smiled as her mother reached out and tousled the stranger's hair, as if he were no more than a willful boy.

He chuckled at her gesture, and she said, "I will not hear another word of it. And if it continues to worry you…well, I'm certain you will have the chance to do something for us one day."

"It will be my only consolation, madam," he said.

Lily rose and retrieved their father's shirt from the floor. Unfolding it, she held it up to Ridge's chest.

Clicking her tongue and shaking her head, she said, "I'm afraid he will be unable to even attempt to wear Father's shirt, Mother."

"So it would seem," Tempest said, smiling.

"If it does not offend you, madam," Ridge began—and Ember sensed his question. She frowned, grimaced with empathy, for she knew it would cause her mother pain. "Where is your husband?"

Tempest forced a smile, though Ember saw the pain in her eyes.

"Lost at sea, darling," she answered simply. "More than fourteen years ago."

"I feared something the like of it. I'm sorry, madam," Ridge mumbled, frowning.

"Thank you. But I have our girls, and we are happy here in our little seaside cottage existence," Tempest added.

"He is there," Ember said, pointing to the painting of her father hanging above the hearth and mantel. "It is his exact likeness, for Lily painted it from memory some years ago."

Ridge West looked up to the painting. The sun had risen, sending warm yellow light beaming into the room. Ember gazed at the painting a moment, her heart aching for missing her father so terribly.

Ridge studied the painting. Ember smiled, knowing her father had been a handsome man. He boasted dark eyes (a gift he'd given to his youngest daughter), strong lines to a strong face, and broad shoulders. Ember's heart warmed at the thought of him—at the memory of his holding her tiny hand as they walked the shore together gathering treasures of the sea.

"He looks to have been a fine man," Ridge said.

"Yes," Tempest sighed.

"And his image captured by a skilled artist, indeed," he added, smiling at Lily.

"Thank you, sir," Lily said—ever gracious, ever graceful, and perfectly lovely.

Suddenly, Ember was aware that she'd spent the night on the floor—that she hadn't combed her hair the entirety of the previous day or night. What a sight she must be—especially in comparison with Lily!

"Perhaps you would allow me to make a sketch or two of you, Mr. West," Lily said then.

"Oh, Lily!" Ember sighed. "The poor man wants only the price of a telegram and a few clothes! Do you really think it's fair to force him to pose for you? I swear my back still aches from the last time I sat all the month long in being sketched."

"All the month long?" Lily breathed, rolling her eyes with exasperation. "It was hardly all the month long!"

"I think it's a fine idea," Tempest said. "After all, where can you roam without fitting trousers and in your state of fatigue, Mr. West? You may as well help Lily perfect her skills in art."

Ember frowned at her mother. Oh, she was not so worried about Ridge's discomfort as Lily's owning his attention for the length of time it would take to make her sketches.

Quickly, Ember bit the inside of her cheek. She was being ridiculous—childish. This was a stranger, a man who had simply washed up on the shore. She owned no claim to him in any way. She owned no attachment to him, other than a feeling of responsibility. She silently told herself the man meant no more to her than the wounded gull that she had found the week before. She'd brought the gull home, placed it in a box, and set it by the fire, tending to it all through the night. What was the difference between a strange man and that gull?

One glance at the handsome man, however, and she knew the difference. Yet it did not change the fact that he was simply a stranger passing through their lives—that she had no legitimate or sane reason to feel the things she was feeling.

"Until my debts are paid, I am your servant, Mrs. Taffee," Ridge said. He glanced to Lily and added, "And yours, Miss Taffee."

Ember's heart quickened its pace as his gaze fell to her then. She could see the sincere gratitude in his eyes as he said, "And most certainly yours, Miss Ember."

Nervously, Ember combed her long hair back with her fingers. She felt her soft, wavy locks cascade over her back—thought how truly wild and unkempt she must appear. Furthermore, a feeling of melancholy, some sort of fearful anxiety, was beginning to surge through her. These sensations were all too familiar, and she would not have them. She would not!

Forcing a smile to her face, she returned Ridge West's gaze. "I suppose I should ready for the day," she said. "I'm glad you're mending, sir," she told him, adding a pleasant lilt to her voice. "I hope your neck does not become too stiff in sitting for the hours necessary for Lily to sketch you."

Ridge's broad brow puckered slightly. He looked to Lily and asked, "Do you mean to sketch me now?"

"Oh, certainly!" Lily chimed. "After all, you look so wild and adventurous after your ordeal! I must capture it before you fully recover and the appearance is vanished!"

"You most surely must," Ember said, smiling and rising to her feet. She looked to the window—to the bright sunshine and blue sky beyond. She sighed and smiled. "I'm glad you're well, Ridge West," she said, glancing to the man sitting on the floor. And it was true. She thought in that moment of what a profound loss it would've been to the world had such a beautiful man been taken to the bottom of the sea. "And I'm glad I found you…even if you won't fit in a bottle on the mantel," she teased.

She bent, kissing Lily on the cheek, and then went to her mother and bestowed the same affection on her. "I think I'll walk the shore, just very quickly if it's all right with you, Mother. Then I promise to wash and dress and be about whatever you ask."

"Of course, darling," Tempest said, smiling, "though I doubt you'll find anything so exciting on the sand as what you found yesterday."

Ember giggled and Lily smiled too, although she was nearly certain Ridge blushed a shade.

"Oh, I'm certain I will not," Ember said. "But at least I might find something that will fit in a bottle."

Ridge smiled and chuckled slightly as the girl smiled at him and winked. He liked her for her sense of humor, if nothing else—although it was obvious there was plenty else to like about her. As she left the cottage, an odd sensation washed over him—as if something had been plucked from his chest, leaving a dark and empty sort of void in its place.

He was beholden to her—that was it. If not for Ember Taffee, he might well have expired there on the sand. He determined then and there that he would find a way to repay her—and her mother and sister.

"Are you ready then?" Lily asked.

"Ready?" Ridge asked, already having forgotten he was to be sketched.

"For me to begin sketching," she explained.

"Oh! Of course," he replied—though he felt the least like being sketched than almost anything. "However, may I be about finding the privy first?"

Tempest laughed, and Ridge was amused as well when Lily's face blushed three deepening shades of crimson.

"It's just out back and to the north, darling," Tempest told him. She frowned, concern obvious on her face. "Will you be able to manage it, do you think?"

"Yes, Mrs. Taffee. Thank you," he assured her, amused as Lily blushed several more hues of crimson.

The sea air was invigorating, and Ridge felt a sum of his strength returned. As he walked to the privy, he glanced to the sea. She was there—his little rescuer. She was walking along the shore, barefoot, hair blowing in the morning breeze. He hoped she found something lovely in the sand—an unusual shell, perhaps an old coin, a pretty something she could put in a bottle.

CHAPTER THREE
TO CLAIM THE VENUS KISS

Ember looked over her shoulder to the cottage. She watched Ridge straddle the ridgepole of the cottage roof, mending it where the wind had damaged it the night before. Her stomach felt as if it were a hotcake being flipped over and over in a hot skillet. What if he slipped—fell? She couldn't watch him, too rattled by the danger posed. Visions of him tumbling off the roof to certain injury plagued her. Thus, she turned and began walking along the water's edge once more.

Still, she'd learned that Ridge West was nothing if not determined and honorable. He'd continually demanded the necessity of somehow repaying Ember's mother for the tiny sum she'd lent him to send a telegram and for the two sets of clothes she'd insisted on purchasing for him. Yet Ember wondered what it would take for such a man to feel his debt had truly been paid. It had been more than a week since Ember had found him on the shore, and already he'd split enough wood to last all winter. Already he'd fixed everything needing fixing in the cottage. Ridge had been so thorough in his work that Ember surmised her mother might never have need of hiring anyone to fix anything ever again.

Furthermore, all he did for them he did before or after he worked for the merchant Morgan. Ridge rose well before the sun and retired long after the women of the cottage. Ember wondered at his stamina—his ambition. She also wondered how it was that a man who had washed up on the shore with not a penny on his person had managed to convince the merchant Morgan to hire him. Damian Morgan was no man to be trifled with. There was not a less gullible or less compassionate man in the world, and yet Ridge had managed to secure employment from him—not simply employment, but employment as a trade negotiator! Tempest, Lily, and Ember had stood mouths gaping in astonishment when Ridge had informed them of his securing a means of earning wages with Morgan. They'd nearly fainted when he told them he would be negotiating trade.

With the promise of wages to be earned, Ridge had also managed to secure a room at the inn in town, though it would not be vacant for another week. In truth, Ember had been sorely disappointed by this news. There was something ever so wonderful about knowing Ridge was in the cottage at night. The awareness offered not only an unfamiliar sort of delight but also a true sense of security—a sense of safety Ember had not known since the sea had taken her father so many years before. She found she was rather nervous about his leaving—disappointed to the very center of her soul. Still, as Lily had said and continued to say, Ridge was not something she could keep in a bottle on the mantel—though the vision of it had begun to be the stuff of her dreams. Often Ember would dream of Ridge—that he was indeed in a bottle, that she could gaze at him to the measure of her own contentment. She'd even begun to dream that she was in the bottle with him—and that when she was in the bottle with him, they were not confined but rather lingered in an existence of beautiful seashore and bright sunshine.

Ember stooped to pick up a pretty shell lying half buried in the sand. She studied it for a moment, trying to divert her thoughts. It was the thoughts of her dreams of a bottled-up Ridge West that were nesting in her mind now, for such dreams she had never known before! She tried not to think of the delicious, romantic nature of them—of how, while dreaming of being inside the beautiful seashore bottle with Ridge, she always found herself in his arms, longing for his kiss, her heart pounding as wild as the storm-driven surf. Even at the thought of the dream, her arms prickled with goose bumps! She silently scolded herself, branding herself a wanton woman, for she did not understand her nearly obsessive attraction to the stranger she'd found on the shore. Certainly she understood she was instinctively drawn to him—drawn to him as surely as if he were some magical creature, spinning a cupidity of desire and delight over her. Yet her common sense told her she was daft. It was insanity to be so preoccupied with dreaming of a man she hardly knew—wicked to own such wanton physical attraction! Furthermore, it was pure madness that her heart was so affected—her heart, which knew better than to dwell on notions that breathtaking romance and true love actually existed.

She stooped, plucking another tiny shell from the sand. She thought for a moment that nothing she would ever find on the shore would look so beautiful in a bottle as would Ridge West—even mermaid tears. Ember sighed, resisting the urge to glance back to the cottage. If she did not look back to Ridge, perhaps her mind would at last be distracted. Still, though she did not look back, she knew that whether or not she did, her thoughts would not waver. She'd been unable to think of anything else since seeing him struggle from the sea and onto the sand. Ridge West had possessed her soul somehow, and she wondered if it would ever be free again.

Ridge paused, exhaled a deep breath, and gazed to the horizon. In truth, he did not gaze to the horizon but rather to the margin just below it—to the seaside—watching Ember carelessly meander along the shore. He'd never known such protective feelings as the girl summoned in him—never. Not even Daisy and Artie provoked such feelings of protectiveness in him as Ember Taffee did. It baffled him, in truth. Certainly, she was a beautiful young woman. Any man would be a liar who declared she did not provoke a lustful appetite. Yet her sister was beautiful too—an opposite sort of beauty, but indeed a beauty in her own right. Therefore, Ridge determined it was not her beauty that drew him to feelings of responsibility toward her safety. Furthermore, she was not weak. Certainly not! Fully capable, ever cheerful, and witty, Ember Taffee was not weak. Yet there was an intangible sense of defenselessness about her—an ethereal sort of vulnerability he could nearly taste. Ridge determined this soft vulnerability was what drew his sense of offering a sort of silent, knightly defense.

For a week he'd lingered, morning and evening, in finding tasks to keep himself busy about the cottage. When he wasn't negotiating trade for Morgan, he was there, ever watchful of Ember, ever as helpful to Tempest and Lily as he could be. Still, it unsettled him that he was drawn to Ember—driven by an almost bewitching need to keep her in his company.

In truth, he'd regretted committing to the room at the inn. Though he would linger another week at the cottage before taking up residency at the inn, Ridge resented the restraints of propriety that had prompted him to seek out the room. Given the choice, he would've stayed at the cottage—would've stayed near to Ember. Yet he knew the filthy minds of gossips, and he would not subject his three ladies of benevolence to such scandal as keeping an unmarried man under their roof any longer might breed. Thus, he would live apart from them—from her. He would visit each evening for supper, as Tempest had demanded, but he would no longer sleep knowing Ember was in the next room. And this caused him to feel worrisome and anxious somehow.

He mused that it was simply the great debt he owed her—the debt of his life. He'd read of people dwelling across the sea who would commit their eternal servitude to one who had saved their life, and he wondered if it were simply this knowledge that caused him to feel so protective of Ember. Perhaps his soul merely knew its debt, that he would've died if she had not found him. Yet he knew there was more—much more—something that he did not like to think on. He was a man, after all. He thought of that morning at breakfast—how his mouth had begun to water as he'd watched Ember take a bite of warm, buttered bread. Such an urge had come over him—an urge to reach across the table, take hold of the front of her blouse, and pull her to him in blending his mouth with her own—that he'd had to quit looking at her altogether! But this was only lust—

substantiation of his carnal desires—or so he surmised, for such a physical covetousness had never been so strong in him.

She stooped, no doubt to pick up something Neptune had strewn in her path. He smiled, thinking it was another little trifle he liked about her—the way she referred to the sea and its god as if she truly still believed in such myths and fairy tales. In the end, Ember Taffee was simply enchanting—as enchanting as Venus herself.

Ridge chuckled out loud and shook his head, amused he'd begun to think in terms of mythical creatures of deity the way Ember did. He turned his attention back to his work, knowing that busy hands helped to distract a mind tending to linger on things it perhaps should not.

Forcing his thoughts to different venues, he pondered the telegram he'd received from Reginald that morning. He'd been so absorbed in the message contained in the telegram that he'd nearly tripped over the poor vagabond—the old sea dog sitting to one side outside of the telegraph office.

"Poor fellow," Ridge mumbled, remembering the tattered, ragged condition of the man. It was not merely his clothes that were worn either but also his body. He was missing one leg from the knee down, as well as a finger. Guilt over nearly having stepped on him had combined with compassion, and Ridge had promised the old sea dog an alms of coin as soon as his first wages were paid him. The kind old fellow had thanked him, assuring him coin was not necessary. Still, Ridge would drop several coins in the poor fellow's hand as soon as Morgan paid him—or when Reginald finally arrived—whichever was first.

He thought of Reginald then, his solicitor and good friend. There was not a finer man on earth than Reginald Oakley. Ridge was grateful for such a loyal friend. Reginald had understood Ridge's instruction to the letter and proceeded as instructed—and in secret. Furthermore, Reginald was in full support of Ridge's decision concerning the direction he had chosen in life. Reginald craved the ability to make the same decision Ridge had, and Ridge hoped that one day he would find the path to doing so.

Ridge smiled, closed his eyes, and inhaled a deep breath of sea air. Yes, life was meant to be challenging—even difficult. But he knew that this was the only way to live a life—through hard work, adversity, and humble joy. He thought then that all he lacked in perfecting the life he had chosen was owning the warm heart and body of a loving woman and children he would love far differently and much more than he was loved.

He growled a light profanity, for the thought had returned his musings to Ember. He determined she was Venus masquerading as the daughter of a woman living in humble circumstance—or in the very least a daughter of the goddess of beauty, love, and fertility doing so.

He growled once more, silently scolding himself, for his thoughts of Ember had again caused his mouth to water.

☙

"Hello, Lily," Ember greeted.

Lily startled, shoving something beneath her skirt. Ember's curiosity was instantly piqued! Lily rarely visited the cove of Mermaid Rock. To find her sitting at its base, quickly concealing something beneath her skirt, was quite intriguing indeed.

"What are you hiding, Lily?" Ember asked plainly.

"Nothing that would interest you, darling," Lily said.

Lily smiled, her eyes twinkling with delight. Ember wondered if perhaps she'd simply been sketching, though Lily rarely sketched the sea. She much preferred portraiture. With this renewed realization, Ember felt a twinge of jealousy prick her heart. Was Lily once again going over her sketches of Ridge? It seemed she sketched nothing or no one else since he'd arrived.

Ember studied her sister's countenance—the sheer beauty of her appearance. She'd always envied Lily, envied her grace and remarkable beauty. It had been one reason she'd been so drawn to Selkirk, for Selkirk had been the one young man in the village who had flirted first with Ember before Lily.

Oh, Ember loved Lily—desperately loved her—and the fact made her occasional envy even more unbearable.

"Are you still sketching Ridge then?" Ember asked, unable to fully suppress the hated envy in her.

"Ridge?" Lily said. "Don't you mean your merman?"

Ember frowned. Her heart began to pound with angst and worry. "What are you talking about, Lily?" she asked. "I found him on the shore. That cannot be changed."

Lily smiled, her emerald eyes glittering with mischief.

Giggling, Lily reached beneath her skirt and produced Ember's diary.

Ember gasped and felt her face blush vermilion. "My diary!" she breathed.

"Yes," Lily sighed, opening the diary. "You really must be more careful with it, Ember," she said. "Why…why, anyone might happen upon it. What if Ridge had been the one to open it, to read your thoughts of having found a merman on the sand, when in truth it was he?"

"You read it?" Ember cried.

Lily shrugged. "Only a little," she admitted, "though I will say this part is quite my favorite." She turned the pages, coming to a stop and smiling. "Ah…here it is. *He is entirely the full measure of the perfect man, this Ridge West sent to us from the sea. When first I saw him, I thought him so faultless in his features and form that I was certain for a moment that Neptune himself had sent him to me, that the most comely son of Neptune, the most handsome and desirable of the merfolk, had been washed to shore at my feet. He is tall, dark-haired, and blue-eyed…and I think him the most attractive man to have ever walked the earth. There is more, for he seems to own some strange hold over me…as if he has enchanted me somehow. Even his voice affects me as to cause me to—*"

Lily's reading ceased as Ember cried, "Give it to me!"

Ember reached for the book, but Lily pulled it away.

"Ember," Lily began, "I wish you wouldn't be so vexed. You know how I love to read your pretty thoughts! They are the stuff of dreams and happiness, the stuff I would have your heart linger upon…instead of…"

"They're not meant for you!" Ember said, choking back tears. "They're my private thoughts. You should not have read them. Mother told you not to the last time you—"

"Oh, please don't be angry with me, Ember," Lily said. She rose and placed a hand on her sister's cheek. "I only like to know you are…that you are moving forward."

"I am moving forward, Lily," Ember said. "Everyone moves forward. It is unavoidable."

Lily's eyes narrowed. "I'm glad he came," she said. "I'm glad he washed up on the sand at your feet. Perhaps he'll draw you fully from the past…draw your heart from continuing to break over that boy. Your girl's heart was broken, Ember. Let your woman's heart see how fully a man can fill it."

"Selkirk *was* a man," Ember reminded. After all, hadn't Selkirk been one and twenty when he'd broken Ember's heart?

"Not a man like Ridge," Lily said. "And well I do not have to tell you that," she said, holding Ember's diary toward her.

Ember snatched the diary, shoving the small book into her apron pocket.

"Try him, Ember," Lily said. "Coax his affections, ask him to kiss you…and then tell me if there is not a difference between a man like Ridge West and a boy like Selkirk Beacon."

"Ask him to kiss me?" Ember gasped. She felt her cheeks burn crimson.

Lily shrugged. "Why not? After all, it's what you dream of…isn't it?" she said, nodding toward Ember's apron pocket.

"Perhaps I do!" Ember defended then. "And what do you dream of, Lily? Don't you own dreams that there might still be one man on this earth who can love a woman as desperately as you and I would love?"

Lily's eyes narrowed, the twinkling joy from a moment before vanishing. "Oh, certainly I dream of it, Ember," she said, "though I know it to be the rarest commodity on earth. Father taught me that it does exist, for he loved Mother that way…as fully as she so desperately loved him. Yet my true sire taught me of the sure rarity of desperate love, for he did not love Mother…nor did he love me."

Ember did not speak; the pain in her heart was too sharp—not the hurt of Lily's betrayal at having read her diary but the tenderness of knowing Lily's pain. Ember and Lily's mother had been married once before, before she married Ember's father. Tempest Taffee's first husband had been a cruel, unfeeling man—a man who neither loved his wife and daughter nor provided that they should be cared for upon the occasion of his death. In all Ember's misery of a broken heart, she knew that Lily's was as deep—different, perhaps, but as thoroughgoing as her own.

"Kiss your son of Neptune, Ember," Lily said. "Then you will know the difference between a man the like of Ridge West and a pitiful boy like Selkirk Beacon. Perhaps then your heart will be healed enough to know that some love might be better than none."

"And you are so experienced in men and boys, Lily?" Ember asked. Her pity had begun to give way to hurt and anger once more.

Lily shrugged. "I've known both…kissed two or three of each." She frowned then, her eyes moist with tears. "Though I do know…it is better to know some love than none."

Ember brushed a tear from her cheek. "You should not have read my thoughts without first asking my permission."

A smile tugged at the corners of Lily's mouth. "Would you have truly let me read it, if I had asked?"

Ember reached into her apron pocket and retrieved her small diary. She offered it to Lily. "Perhaps…given the chance." She again offered the diary to her sister. "Take it. Take it and know my pretty thoughts, as you call them. I have nothing to hide from you, Lily," she said. "You know my heart was broken by Selkirk Beacon. You know I find Ridge West the most attractive man you or I have ever seen. But it changes nothing…for further you know that I do not believe Neptune washed him onto the shore for my benefit."

"Perhaps you should believe it," Lily said, accepting the diary.

Ember saw Lily's gaze shift. Her sister no longer gazed at her but looked beyond her as if something of more interest was at her back.

"Good evening, Ridge," Lily said then.

"Good evening, Lily," he greeted, adding, "Good evening, Ember," when Ember turned to see Ridge striding toward them. "Have you ladies found any treasures on your walk today?" he asked.

Oh, he was more handsome than Adonis! Ember was aware she was holding her breath, as ever awed at the sudden sight of him.

"Not so many," Lily answered when Ember did not. "Though I have been doing some interesting reading," Lily said, indicating the book in her hand.

"Yes?" Ridge asked, reaching for the book.

"No!" Ember gasped, slapping his hand away. His brow puckered in a puzzled frown.

"It's her diary, you see," Lily explained. "And I was only just reading of the day she found you." Lily cast a knowing, teasing glance at Ember as she leaned toward Ridge and whispered, "She thought you were a merman when first she saw you. Did you know that?"

Ember thought certain she might drop dead of humiliation and the hurt of betrayal. But somehow, Ridge's soft, low chuckle kept her heart from stopping.

"Is that so?" he asked, smiling at her.

"Ask her to tell you about it, Ridge," Lily said, moving past him. "It's really a very interesting story." She was gone then, Ember's diary still in her hand.

When Lily had gone further up the shore, Ridge turned to Ember. She felt her cheeks blazing and struggled to keep the tears of humiliation from escaping her eyes.

"Is that true?" he asked.

Ember gulped, speechless. How could she confess she'd entertained such ridiculous musings?

"Did she really read your diary?" he asked then. "Without your permission?"

Ember drew an astonished breath. Was he not astonished at what Lily had revealed?

"Y-yes," she stammered.

Ridge shook his head, clicking his tongue with disapproval. "And she appears so well mannered...so refined."

Ember smiled, delighted by his chivalry. He was trying to distract her from her own embarrassment by feigning disinterest in the contents of her diary. This warmed her heart—fairly set it aflame—and she did not deny in that moment that Ridge had soothed the break in it—if only a little.

"And now I'm ready to be teased," she said. It was true. Because he had been so kind, so heroic in not teasing her about what Lily had revealed the contents of her diary to be, she fairly *wanted* him to tease her. Furthermore, though she'd known him only a week, she well knew he was in possession of a great sense of humor.

He smiled, his blue eyes shimmering with mirth. The sight of his smile—his beautiful eyes—his purely ethereal presence caused Ember to feel breathless and weak.

"Well, I really can't decide if I'm flattered...or offended," Ridge said.

"Offended?" Ember asked.

Ridge was amused by the sincere confusion apparent on her pretty face. Did she really not see why a man might be offended at being compared to a fish?

He smiled and said, "Mermen, they seem...well...the idea seems...to me it seems they'd be rather too feminine for me to be flattered at your thinking I was one."

Ember giggled, her onyx eyes glistening with mirth. She shook her head, still amused. He knew her sister had hurt her—vexed her in the very least by reading her private thoughts penned to paper. Yet he felt the need to protect her from further pain. Thus, he would tease her. After all, it was fast becoming one of his favorite entertainments.

"Oh, but you should be more flattered than ever you have been," she explained, her eyes brightening even further. He'd soothed her, and the playful imp in her character he so adored was skipping about.

"I should?"

Ember nodded. "Of course you should, for mermen are the handsomest creatures, with the broadest shoulders and such profound musculature that they look to have been sculpted from pure granite!"

Ridge chuckled. "Oh, now I'm certain of it!"

"Certain of what?" Ember asked.

"Certain you want something of me," he answered. "Handsome, musculature like sculpted granite? You want something of me, or else you're simply trying to make me feel better for having thought I was a fish when first you found me."

"Oh no!" Ember exclaimed, placing a hand on his shoulder. "It's true! They're the handsomest of creatures, in face and form! Oh, I know mermen aren't real, of course, but if they were, you would be the perfect one." She paused, glancing to his legs. "Only you'd have a fin...instead of legs, of course."

"Of course!" He laughed wholeheartedly then. Oh, he knew she was sincere; he knew she thought he was attractive, and he was glad—very glad. Yet the devil in him was afoot, and he would tease her awhile yet. After all, what man would not delight in having a pretty young woman reassure him of his good looks?

"So what is it you want of me?" he teased.

"Oh, nothing...truly!" Ember assured him. "I truly only had the fancy that you would make a perfect merman...if they existed. When I found you on the shore, I'd been searching for more mermaid tears...looked up, saw you, and naturally had the fleeting thought..."

"That a merman had washed ashore," he finished.

"Yes." She smiled at him.

"What do you want, Ember Taffee?" he continued to tease.

"Nothing! Truly!" she begged him to believe, placing a warm palm against the bareness of his chest. At her touch, Ridge felt goose bumps ripple over his arms. He should not be so affected by her touch—but he was.

He pretended to be thoughtful a moment and then asked, "Are mermen...are they like their counterparts...like mermaids in every way?"

Ember's pretty brows puckered with puzzlement. "Well, they are mer*men* and not maids," she offered.

Ridge fought in keeping his expression to appear serious. Ember was so delightfully, unintentionally humorous! He had to clench his teeth to keep from smiling and laughing at her. "No, I mean, mermaids...they own a siren's song, yes?" he asked.

"Yes," she answered, obviously curious.

"Well then, do mermen own something the like? Can mermen seduce women the way mermaids do men?" he asked.

"Yes...or so I was always told," she answered.

Suddenly, a curiosity entered Ridge's mind, and he asked, "So you were told? By whom?"

Instantly, he regretted asking the question, for a shadow clouded Ember's dark eyes, and she gazed to the horizon beyond the sea. "My father," she answered. "It was my father who told me all the tales of the merfolk. I was very small...only five when he was lost," she explained. "But I remember every story of mermaids and mermen he ever told me. We used to walk along the shore together, searching for mermaid tears—sea glass. We used to search for sea glass together."

He sensed a melancholy in her and silently scolded himself for being the cause of it. "So it was the stories your father told you that caused you to think I was a merman when you looked up and saw me washed up on the shore," he offered, attempting to lighten the course of their conversation once more.

Whether for his attempts at lightening her spirits or for the sake that Ember was simply a cheerful person, her eyes glistened brightly again, and she said, "Yes."

"I think I'm not so offended at your comparing me to a merman as I was at first," he sighed. "After all, by your measure I'm the handsomest of creatures, with the body wrought of a master sculptor, and..." He paused, grinning at her mischievously. "And with the power to seduce women with simply the sound of my voice."

Ember's heart began to quicken its pace as Ridge's eyes narrowed, as his teasing smile turned to an alluring grin.

"Shall we put me to the test?" he asked. "Shall we see if I have the power of the merfolk? Shall we see if I can seduce you with merely the sound of my voice and my words?"

"Alas...I am not seducible," she told him. And she was not. She knew she was not. Ember had been seduced once before—certainly not to immorality, but seduced of the heart—and she would not be so willing and weak again.

"Aren't you?" Ridge asked. Ember fancied the deep blue of his eyes endeavored to mesmerize her somehow.

"No," she told him. Yet she was not so certain of herself as she had been a moment before.

"Pity," he said, his voice low, rich, and deep like some dark, decadent confection, "for I am certain your kiss would taste sweeter than sugared berries."

Ember quivered as Ridge trailed the back of one hand over the bareness of her arm—slowly caressed her from her wrist to her shoulder. She suddenly wished she'd worn a longer sleeve, for his touch was nearly unbearable in its effect on her.

"Is your kiss that sweet, Ember Taffee?" he asked.

Ember's heart was madly pounding! Her mouth suddenly flooded with moisture—warm desire and longing. She studied Ridge's face a moment, her gaze lingering on his lips. She thought his kiss might be the stuff of dreams, but she could not allow herself to know. She would not allow herself to know. Lily's encouragement that she ask him to kiss her entered her mind, accompanied by every dream she'd ever dreamt of him.

She shrugged and, feigning indifference, sighed, "I don't know. Perhaps...perhaps not."

"I could sample it for you," he lured. "Just a sample. That's all it would take for me to know if your mouth is truly as sweet as the appearance of it promises to be."

"Yes...you could," Ember told him, again feigning strength and indifference. "Still, if my kiss is not as sweet as sugared berries, then you will know great disappointment, which, in turn, might cause your siren's power to wane."

"Your kiss could never disappoint," he said.

Ember winced slightly, for she knew—deep in the damaged portion of her heart, she knew—that indeed her kiss could well disappoint. "You don't know that," she mumbled.

"Then put it to the test," he dared. "Let me decide whether seducing you is worth exhausting my siren's song."

Ember's gaze lingered on his lips again—lingered on his perfect, tempting lips. Again excess moisture—desire—flooded her mouth. Perhaps her kiss was not so repulsive as she had grown to think. Perhaps her feminine allure had grown since last she'd wagered her heart and lost. Furthermore, the part of her that had been vexed by Lily's provoking begged defense.

"Very well, son of Neptune," she told him—though her breath caught a moment after she'd said it.

"Very well?" he asked, obviously surprised.

"Y-yes," she stammered, attempting to appear unflustered. "Your siren's song has worked its spell. I am utterly in your power."

"Hmm. Wonderful," Ridge breathed.

Ridge smiled, though he could sense she was near terrified. He did not know why she was so unsettled—just that she was. Still, she had taken his bait, and he could not release her now, lest she think he did not truly want to kiss her. Mostly he could not release her for the sake of so wantonly wanting to kiss her that his mouth was watering—desperate to know her taste.

Smiling, Ridge slipped a strong hand beneath her hair to the back of her neck. At once, his touch caused Ember to tremble, and she silently scolded herself for being so weakened by his teasing. She wondered for a brief moment if he truly did possess the gift of a siren's song, for she found she could not have run from him if all her very will had wanted to—which it did not.

She was surprised, and painfully disappointed, when he did not kiss her immediately. Rather she felt his hand at the back of her neck move—felt his fingers weave into her hair—felt him fist her hair, tugging at it gently until her head fell back to expose the length of her vulnerable throat. She gasped and held her breath as she felt his other hand at her throat, resting on the curve of it for a time, his thumb caressing the hollow.

"You humans have very soft skin," he mumbled.

She could not help but smile at his teasing, even for the trembling induced in her body by his intimate touch.

"I like this space here," he said as his thumb lingered in the hollow of her throat. His voice was low, soothing, alluring. The sound and quality of it calmed her so, that she did not startle when he said, "I think I'll begin here…just here where your skin is so soft…soft and velvet like a rose petal. Though I do imagine your mouth to be just as pleasing."

One powerful hand still woven and fisted in her hair, his other traveled over her arm—to her waist—to linger on the small of her back as she felt his lips press lightly against the hollow of her throat. Twice he pressed his warm kiss to the tender, sensitive place, stealing her breath, sending her heart to pound erratically. A third time he kissed the space, and she felt this kiss was laced with warm moisture, as if he'd actually tasted her skin while kissing her. His hand in her hair relaxed as he carefully kissed her throat—her chin—her jaw just below her ear.

Ridge wanted to simply crush his mouth to hers—claim the Venus kiss. That's what he'd wanted to do; that's how he wanted to kiss her. Yet instinct had directed him to an easement where Ember was concerned—an instinct that seemed heightened somehow. He couldn't simply take her mouth the way his desire drove him to. Not this time—not the first time. Yes, this was simply the first time he would know the taste of her skin—of her mouth—of that he was determined. The thought caused him to smile, even for his endeavors to bewitch the girl with his slow, titillating applications of affection.

This would not be a singular event; this would not be the once he would kiss her—no! He hadn't even sampled her mouth yet, and already he knew he would be driven to taste her again!

She was trembling in his arms. Was she delighted—or frightened? He thought perhaps both. Carefully, he took her face between his hands—directed her lips to meet his. He thought for a moment that he might not be able to manage his desires, for her kiss was so soft and sweet as to tease with every sense in his body. She accepted this tender kiss from him—reciprocated—and he pressed her further, releasing a ragged breath as her lips parted, allowing a more intimate melding of mouths.

Ember shuddered as bright, colorful beams of light burst through her mind—as warmth and desire coursed through her veins. She could not discern whether it was the crash of the surf ringing in her ears or the mad pounding of her heart as it pumped her blood with the force of repetitive cannon blasts!

Suddenly she could not keep her hands from finding his face. The feel of his jaw working as he kissed her—of his whisker stubble scratching her palm as well as the flesh around her mouth—only served to increase her trembling, her euphoria, and her desire! He gathered her in his powerful arms, pulling her body tight against his as he continued to direct their kiss. Ember's own arms went around his neck, her hands knowing bliss in the feel of his soft hair between her fingers.

She was lost—utterly lost in the flames of desire! There was no ocean, no cottage, no one else in all the world! In that moment, there was only him—the handsome seducer, Ridge West. His mouth worked such a spell of warm, moist, flavorful passion that Ember was certain it was not at all natural—not humanly anyway! Only some mythical creature could evoke such desire in her—kiss her as if he were the only man she was ever meant to kiss.

And then—then it happened. Ember's heart remembered pain. The memory of heartbreak erupted through her body as if someone had plunged a dagger straight into the center of her chest. And yet never had Selkirk kissed her this way. Never had such feelings of desire pounded her body the way the sea pounded the rocks near the shore. She felt it—her heart melding to the man in whose arms she lingered—and she knew. She knew she could love this man as she'd never loved Selkirk Beacon—and loving Selkirk Beacon had nearly killed her! Selkirk Beacon had been but a puff of breath on her cheek compared with the raging wind Ridge West was commanding. Pain! Disappointment! Agony! It was what awaited her if she surrendered her heart to him.

Ridge felt Ember stiffen in his arms, felt her body shudder with what seemed a tremor born of fear. Oh, he did not want to give her up! He did not want to forfeit the warm pleasure of her mouth. Yet he sensed the panic in her and quickly broke the seal of their lips. Gazing into the dark pools of her eyes, he saw the trepidation in them and again wondered what caused such a beautiful, confident, and playful young woman to own such terror.

Still, he would champion her—keep from frightening her further. He would protect her as best he could.

"Uh oh," he said.

"What?" Ember asked. She was certain she would melt into tears and sobbing at any moment. Yet she did not want Ridge to know the feelings in her—not her remembered heartache at the hand of Selkirk Beacon nor the knowledge only just affirmed to her that Ridge West could own her without so much as another touch.

"My legs," he said, frowning. "They feel strange. I…I think I'm sprouting a fin! I think I might be a girlie merman after all!"

Ember glared at him but could not help but smile. She playfully slapped his broad, firm chest and pushed herself from his arms.

"I told you already. Mermen aren't girlie," she giggled. "They're…they're bulking, handsome, and very masculine."

"They're probably more girlie than some girls I've known, Ember," he argued as she turned and started up the shore toward the cottage.

Lily smiled as she heard Ember laugh. Ridge West was the one—she was certain of it now! Neptune had sent him—washed him ashore to heal her sister's broken heart. And, oh, how he would heal it.

Lily hugged herself, chafing her arms against the cooling evening air as she watched Ember and Ridge walking toward home. She felt bad for reading her sister's private thoughts—felt devilish for baiting her with the pretense that she'd never known the kiss of a man. Yet she knew Ember—knew her vexation would cause her to be curious. Furthermore, Ridge had complied with Lily's wishes, even though he knew nothing of them. What man wouldn't want to comfort Ember Taffee when she was hurt or disappointed? And Ridge West tended toward chivalry far more than any other man Lily had ever met.

Yes, Ridge would drive Selkirk Beacon from Ember's mind and heart. Lily was certain he would. After all, why else would Neptune have sent him?

CHAPTER FOUR
CUPIDITY

Sleep was entirely elusive! Ember's mind and body were so affected by the memory—by the lingering bliss provoked by Ridge's kiss—that she could not coax one wink of sleep to attend her. Her thoughts were disorganized, rambling, and often confusing to her heart. Visions of Ridge's handsome face—his smile, the light in his eyes as he listened to her—beautiful visions kept appearing in her mind! Sensations—bliss, warmth, delight—wonderful feelings of hope, joy, and possibility kept resonating through her as if she were some stringed instrument and Ridge had plucked a filament of her being that had never before been in tune with her soul!

It's purely prurient, she thought to herself. What woman could bar herself from a shocking sort of attraction to Ridge West? Yet she did not like to think she was some lurid woman, a woman who could be so affected by the physical. Even with Selkirk she had not known such strong desires, and she had loved him.

For a moment, she was frightened—terrified! Perhaps for the sake of her broken heart, she'd lost more than her desire to love again. Perhaps she'd lost the ability to love! She sat straight up in her bed a moment, thinking of Esmerelda Van Avery, the woman who worked at the drinking establishment in town. A cold, horrified sweat beaded at Ember's forehead as she thought of what was said of the rather loose Esmerelda—that her heart had been broken at the age of sixteen, that she'd vowed never to fall in love again. Esmerelda Van Avery had barred her broken heart to any healing and in barring it had apparently lost the ability to love—though she did seem to enjoy the physical company of men.

"Esmerelda!" Ember gasped. But no! No! She shook her head, knowing she was no such woman as Esmerelda—that she could never be such a woman. Still, she was disturbed by the reality of Ridge's effect on her. Oh, what a kiss she'd shared with him! What a kiss! Ember sighed, overcome with goose bumps and a fluttering sensation in her stomach at the very thought of his kiss.

Briefly she considered—as her imagination ever seemed to—that perhaps there did exist a Neptune or some such like creature who had put Ridge in her path. Yes, perhaps Cupid! Yes! Cupid, Roman god of impassioned love, son of Venus herself. Perhaps Neptune and Cupid had conspired to mend Ember's damaged heart! Perhaps they had sent Ridge to her, knowing that his physical beauty and rare character would capture her attention.

Ember growled, disgusted with her own silly musings. She fluffed her pillow and lay down. Inhaling a deep breath, she slowly exhaled in an attempt to calm herself. She tried to empty her mind—tried to will away the goose bumps on her arms, the fluttering in her stomach. Yet the serenity did not last long, as the vision of Ridge's image returned to her thoughts a hundredfold.

"For pity's sake!" she exclaimed in a whisper. "He's a stranger! I don't know him from some Irishman across the sea."

In that moment, however, she heard her mother's voice tranquilly echoing through her mind. *Every love begins with two strangers*, her mother had told her once.

Long ago—several years after Ember's father had been lost at sea—Ember had asked her mother to tell her the story of how Tempest Alexander had come to wed the Captain Mariner Taffee.

"Every love begins with two strangers, my darling," her mother had begun. "And your father and I, we were strangers…but only for a moment."

Ember's mother had always avowed that she had fallen in love with Captain Taffee the moment her eyes first beheld him. Captain Mariner Taffee had avowed the same. In truth, the love of Mariner and Tempest was still talked about in town—on occasion—and carefully.

Ember herself had once heard one elderly woman tell another, "Theirs was true love, the kind that only comes round the world once in a hundred years!" And Ember believed it. She'd seen it, after all—witnessed her mother and father resplendent in one another's company. She was young when the sea took her father, that was true, but she remembered him well—remembered the love that was so true and substantial in the little cottage by the shore that anyone who entered in could nearly taste it.

"Every love begins with two strangers," Ember whispered. Could it be that the allure—the near wild attraction she felt toward Ridge West—was only the physical manifestation of the true love her soul already knew she would own for him? The thought frightened her, for what if her soul was destined to love him? What if her heart was fated to be his? What if she fell in love with him, only to find that Neptune had been cruel, that Ridge West's heart was not human, that he would not or could not love her in return?

She thought of Selkirk, of what a handsome man he was, of how he'd charmed her—promised his heart belonged only to her. With Selkirk she'd talked of marriage, of a life entwined with his, and he had promised her his whole heart. Selkirk had pledged his love too— sworn he would never love another. And yet he had not been true. One voyage to the south—three weeks—had been all the time it had taken for his heart to adhere to another. Three weeks and the love he'd promised to share with Ember ended. It had taken three weeks for Selkirk to transfer his love and affections to another young woman, but it had only taken a blink for Ember's heart to break.

As the rush of pleasure at remembering Ridge's kiss washed over Ember once more, she began to hum to herself to distract her fevered mind. She hummed an old tune her father had always hummed while tucking her into her bed when she was a child. The song was "The Mariner's Mermaid," and it did soothe her—just as it had when her father had hummed or sang it so long ago.

Ridge lay on this back, staring up through the dim light to the ceiling. He sighed and turned to see the dying embers in the hearth. *Embers*, he thought. *Embers!* He feared he would never find sleep, for his mind and body were far too agitated by thoughts of Ember. Warm embers lay in the hearth; a painting of Ember (her sister's art displayed) hung on one wall; bottles of sea glass and shells (all collected by Ember) lined the mantel. Even the blanket that covered him, Ember had crocheted it, and it carried her fragrant, ambrosial scent!

His mouth flooded with moisture as he thought of her— remembered their kiss. He tried to think of something else—of someone else. He glanced to the sofa and saw Lily's sketchbook lying there. Lily. She was lovely. He would think of her. Dark-haired, emerald-eyed, she was a beauty. Ridge frowned as he wondered then at Lily's rather aloof nature, of her apparent lack of emotional sensitivity. It seemed she was too hardhearted for a woman of such a tender age. He wondered if there was a darkness in her past. Perhaps a man had broken her heart. Perhaps she'd suffered some other tragedy. Whatever the case, it was sure Lily did not own the ethereal beauty of spirit that Ember did. Ember!

Ridge shook his head and tightly shut his eyes, rubbing them with tired hands. Ember! She had become his every thought! Even when he was away from the cottage, in town negotiating trade for the merchant Morgan, even then he would find his mind distracted by thoughts of her!

"Ember," he muttered aloud, intrigued by the way the very pronouncing of her name seemed to warm him, to evoke desire and delight in him.

He sat up, certain he was losing his mind. Oh, he was a man— that part he well understood. What man would not be drawn to her? What man would not experience thoughts of desired intimacy and longing? Still, it was more than that—far more! Ridge could feel obsession lurking just a breath away. Obsession—for a girl he'd known less than a fortnight. It was inconceivable—yet true!

His irrational mind considered for a moment—considered rising, striding into the room where she slept—considered snatching her from her bed and kissing her until he'd felt he had his fill. The difficulty was, he mused, it would take eternity to quench his desire for her kiss—eternity and beyond!

He was glad that his room at the inn was near ready for him to occupy. It would make it easier for him to concentrate on sleep and other necessities of a healthy existence. He'd slept very little since coming to Taffee cottage. Furthermore, when he did sleep, his dreams were so dominated by visions of Ember Taffee that he never felt rested when he woke.

He thought of his father then—wondered if he himself were more like the old shipbuilder than he thought. His father had always been utterly driven by desire—desire of wealth, desire of position, desire of power, not to mention physical desire for beautiful women. He pitied his stepmother for a moment and then remembered it was her own desire for riches that found her married to such a man as his father. Though the pity did return when he thought of her untimely death, of never having been able to see the babies grow up—the babies she'd given her life to bear. He did pity Daisy and Art, for he loved them, and not merely for the half-sister and half-brother they were to him. He pitied them for owning such parents. How he'd like to kidnap them, whisk them away to a full life—the sort of life the Taffee women knew.

Ridge shook his head. He was not like his father—no! Ember had simply worked a spell over him. He wondered for a moment if the Roman gods were real, if their minions truly existed—merfolk with siren's songs. Oh, certainly he'd teased Ember that day, teased her in pretense that he had powers to seduce her. Now, however, he'd begun to wonder if perhaps Ember was a siren of the sea—perhaps her mother and sister as well. Was he simply bewitched my Ember's beauty—by her dark, alluring eyes, her soft, berry-sweet lips, her lilting voice, and her enchanting nature?

There was more that disturbed him as well, for it was not simply his body that desired Ember's company but his heart as well.

Somehow she'd settled there, deep inside it, as if she belonged there—had been at once melded to it! Ridge had never known such a sensation in his chest, such a burn within the organ that pumped his blood. It was this fact that caused him to experience an anxious sort of fear—as if, were he unable to win Ember's heart, his might expire.

"I don't even know the girl!" he mumbled, rubbing his tired eyes once more. He smiled and chuckled with amusement at the sudden memory. "A merman, Ridge!" he chuckled quietly. "She thought you were a merman."

Ridge exhaled a heavy breath of fatigue. He forced his thoughts to the morrow, to the trade meetings, to Reginald's arrival. Perhaps seeing Reginald would distract him. No doubt his friend and solicitor had much information to share. Perhaps their meeting would keep him from such obsessive thoughts as he was battling now.

"A merman," he breathed, still smiling. He turned on his side and gazed into the hearth, its heart warmed by the glowing embers of the dying fire.

"Ember," he breathed.

ॐ

"Something's different," Reginald said.

Ridge smiled and breathed a chuckle as he put his signature to the papers Reginald had laid out for him. "Is that so?" he asked.

"Oh yes," Reginald affirmed, his eyes narrowing as he studied Ridge.

"Well, I've jumped a ship, spent the night in the sea, washed up on the shore in a strange town…" Ridge mumbled, still signing.

"No," Reginald stated. "You've always been up to mischief the likes of that. No, it's something else."

Ridge chuckled, handed Reginald the papers, and watched his friend tuck them into a brown satchel.

"Mischief?" Ridge exclaimed in a whisper.

He did not like sitting in such a dark and dirty establishment as was the Sailor's Knot. But it was exactly because it was dark and rather sparsely populated at midafternoon that Ridge had chosen to meet Reginald there. Glancing about, he saw that the old vagabond sea dog—to whom he'd offered several coins for nearly having stepped on him once before—sat nearby. A man stood behind the bar polishing glasses, and a very painted-looking woman stood near him, though she often let her alluring expression rest on Ridge and his friend.

"Mischief?" Ridge repeated, smiling. "What mischief the likes of jumping ship in the middle of the night have I ever been up to before?"

"You're hiding something, Ridge," Reginald said. He grinned, knowing he was making Ridge uncomfortable. "Tell me what you're hiding, other than your true identity—that you're actually Chamridge Westminster, heir apparent to one of the greatest fortunes ever to be—"

"Sshh!" Ridge scolded. "I'm not hiding anything, Reggie." Ridge paused, shrugged his shoulders, and whispered, "With the sole exception perhaps that…"

"That what?" Reginald urged when Ridge did not continue.

"Do you believe that you or…or any man…do you believe you could actually love someone's soul at once? I mean, instantly," he expounded, "the moment you first meet them?"

Reginald's eyes widened. "Gone a week, and you've already let some pretty thing sticky up your head?"

"No, no," Ridge argued, frowning and shaking his head. He rubbed his eyes—eyes that still burned from lack of sleep. He lowered his voice yet again. "My heart," he confessed. "It's my heart she's testing. Or perhaps even my soul. I swear, sometimes I think she's bewitched me."

Reginald was silent for a moment, obviously thoughtful. His eyes narrowed. "You've never been easy prey for a woman, Ridge. Never. Are you telling me…are you telling me some lovely huntress has finally tracked you to ground?"

"No, no," Ridge mumbled. "Of course not." He paused, looking up to Reginald. "Maybe." He shook his head. "Though she's not a huntress. She's not like the women we know, Reggie. She's sweet, lovely, pure…like some sort of wild angel or…or mer…"

"Or what?" Reginald prodded.

"A mermaid siren come ashore," Ridge muttered.

Reginald grinned. "Oh, I see," he said. "She must be some beauty of myth indeed, if she's got Chamridge Westminster so twisted up."

"Shh," Ridge scolded again.

"And have you...does she know she's your puppeteer?" Reginald asked.

"No. I mean, she's not. No," Ridge stammered. He rubbed at his chin, shrugged his shoulders, and said, "I kissed her yesterday."

"Kissed her?" Reginald chuckled. "What kind of kiss? Was it the old I-think-you're-pretty-so-I'll-steal-me-a-peck kiss?"

Ridge rubbed his chin again, shaking his head slightly.

Reginald's eyebrows arched, his smile broadening once more. "Oh, I see," he said. "More the I'm-the-handsomest-wolf-ever-born-and-I'll-have-my-way-with-you-or-be-hanged sort."

"She's under my skin, Reggie," Ridge growled. "Under my skin, branded into my brain...searing my flesh like I was some lustful, lascivious sort of degenerate."

"All men are lustful sorts, good fellow. At one time or the other...more often than any of us care to admit, I'm afraid."

"This is different," Ridge mumbled. "She owns me. I swear she does! Exactly as if I were her pet dog. And I've only known her a week."

"Linger then. Linger here in this town, and perhaps...perhaps when another week has passed, you won't feel so strange about it."

"One more week and I fear I might find myself proposing marriage to the little mermaid!" Ridge growled.

Reginald shrugged broad shoulders, raking strong hands through his sand-colored hair. "What of it?" he asked. "There's got to be a reason she's woven herself through your soul."

Ridge looked to his friend and smiled. "What the devil are you doing, Reggie?" he asked. He gestured toward the man, to his fine suit. "Still a solicitor? You hate the profession, and I know it."

"I do," he said. "Fact is, I might show up at your inn door begging for help in finding work here." Reginald smiled. "It's done you good! I've never seen you so happy...or so confused!" He laughed, and Ridge smiled. "Your body's strong, your skin is tanned like a sailor's, and I've never seen this much life in your eyes."

"Say the word, Reginald," Ridge said. "Say the word, and I'll speak to the merchant Morgan about you. Perhaps he needs a solicitor...one who doesn't mind a few calluses as well."

Reginald nodded. "I've nearly got Mother provided for," he said. He nodded once more. "I may just do it, Ridge. I may at that."

Ridge watched as he fastened his satchel, pushed his chair back from the table, and stood. He offered a hand to Ridge. Ridge stood, accepting his hand and shaking it firmly.

"I'll take care of this business, Ridge," Reginald said. "The trusts, the sales...I'll get it done."

"Thank you, Reggie," Ridge said.

"Meanwhile, you pull that little mermaid of yours into some secluded cove somewhere and make up your mind whether you're just a lecherous old scoundrel...or a man in love."

"And what if I am just a lecherous old scoundrel?" Ridge asked.

Reginald shrugged. Ridge recognized the teasing mirth glistening in his eyes.

"Then let the angel mermaid loose," he said. "From the way the serving girl in here is looking at you, I'm sure she'd be willing to get to know you better—lecherous old scoundrel or not."

Ridge chuckled and shook his head. "You'll hear from me soon," he told his friend.

"I'll look forward to it," Reginald said.

Ridge watched him leave—watched him nod to the old one-legged sailor seated nearby.

"Good day, sir," Reginald told the man.

"And to you, lad," the old man responded.

Ridge left the dark, rather dreary establishment and started toward the merchant's warehouse. It would feel good to have things finally settled. His mind flitted to Artie and Daisy, and he wondered if they were well, though he knew they were. His father would never neglect their health. One day, he'd return—when they were older, when they could more ably see how different life could be outside the clouded realm of wealth and luxury.

He chuckled to himself as he entered the warehouse, musing at how little Reginald had assisted him in sorting out his feelings where Ember was concerned. All he could think about, even in that moment, was Ember—of seeing her, touching her, tasting her mouth. All he could think of was Ember—Ember Taffee—surely Venus embodied.

He rolled his eyes, nearly laughing out loud then at his own wild contemplations. Venus, the goddess of love and beauty. The goddess Venus had borne Cupid of her dalliance with Mercury. Mercury, the Roman god of merchants, of trade and commerce. As he watched the merchant Morgan, the man for whom Ridge himself negotiated trade and commerce, he smiled.

Rubbing his tired eyes once more, he swallowed the excess moisture flooding his mouth at the thought of kissing Ember.

"You've made me a wealthier man today, Ridge West," Mr. Morgan said. "The entire ship's cargo went for near twice what I thought it would, thanks to you."

"I'm glad you're pleased, Mr. Morgan," Ridge said. "Yet I hope I have not done you a disservice somehow. Wealth wears many masks, riches being the most frightening."

The merchant Morgan chuckled, slapped Ridge on the back, and nodded. "You're wise beyond your years, Ridge," he said. "Wise beyond your years."

Ridge smiled, wondering, if he were so wise, why he could not simply spin out of the spell Ember Taffee was weaving over him.

"And how was your day in trading?" Ember asked. She tried to steady her breath—tried to still her madly pounding heart. Her heart had begun to hammer sorely within her bosom the very moment Ridge had joined her for her evening meander along the shore.

She smiled as the handsome son of the sea god shrugged broad shoulders and answered, "Successful...I suppose."

"You suppose?" Ember giggled.

"Yes, I suppose," he repeated. "Oh!" he exclaimed unexpectedly. "I was so ravenous when I returned this evening that your mother's stew distracted me from remembering this."

Ember smiled as he reached into the pocket of his trousers, frowning as he seemed to be struggling to retrieve something.

"Here," he said, taking her hand and pressing something into the palm of her hand. "For you."

Ember's heart fluttered, her stomach filling with an airy sort of excitement. A gift? He meant to give her something? In that moment, she determined that she didn't care if it was a broken bit of an old pot. She would love it!

She gasped, however, when she looked to see a cobalt piece of sea glass, smoothed near perfectly round by the sea and fashioned with small leather straps and sapphire blue ribbon into a stunning bracelet.

"Oh my goodness!" she breathed as she studied it. "Why ever would you…I can't believe…oh, it's lovely! Simply lovely! I've never seen such a pretty tear, I swear it. Not in all my life of wandering along the shore!"

"There's an old sea dog in town. Perhaps you know him. He's a pretty weathered old sailor, lots of scars on his face and arms. He's got one leg that's stiff and won't bend much. I nearly tripped over him a few days back. I apologized and promised to gift him a coin or two for his trouble…when I finally had a coin or two."

Ember looked to him and smiled, mesmerized by the delight in his beautiful eyes.

"Which I do have now," he said.

"Have what?" she asked, not having heard him—for she'd been thoroughly distracted by his handsome face and dazzling smile, by the sudden leap of her heart.

"I have a coin or two," he repeated. "And I offered the poor fellow I'd stepped on the other day…a coin or two. He wouldn't accept them at first, not until I saw his wares peeking out from his ragged old satchel. I asked him, if he would not accept the alms, would he allow me to purchase something from his stores. He was reluctant at first, but then I told him I knew a pretty girl who favored mermaid tears, and he showed me this."

Ember thought she might weep, truly! Her heart was so swollen with joy, she thought sure it would burst from her chest.

"He had all sorts of things he's fashioned from sea treasures," Ridge continued, "necklaces adorned with tiny shells, other bracelets, hair adornments. But this...this was by far the most appropriate for you. Don't you think?"

She couldn't breathe! In fact, she was so overcome with sheer elation, she placed her free hand to her throat in an attempt to slow the intense emotion rising there. "It's...it's beautiful!" she managed. "I can't believe you would—"

"Here," he said, taking the bracelet from her hand.

Ember watched as Ridge placed it at her wrist, awkwardly securing it with the leather ties meant for the purpose. His touch was too affecting, too wonderful, and she thought she might swoon.

"There," he said at last. "My gift to you, Miss Ember Taffee...my guardian angel."

She could not restrain her enthusiasm then—her pure felicity! Boldly she threw her arms about his neck and embraced him, whispering, "Oh, thank you! It's beautiful. Thank you!"

At the feel of his hands at her waist—as his lips brushed her ear, his warm breath breathing, "You're welcome"—she thought sure she would melt, melt from the delight, desire, and untainted happiness enfolding her in that moment.

She held him a moment more—reveled in the glorious sense of his arms around her, of his breath on her neck. She felt his lips softly press her skin just below her ear and trembled for the thrill it sent racing through her.

Raising herself more unsteadily on the tips of her toes, she kissed his rugged jaw. His whiskers prickled her tender lips, and she smiled, for she liked the sense.

She felt his hands at her waist once more—felt his grip tighten there as if he meant to put her away from him. Instead, she gasped as his mouth suddenly found hers—warm, moist, and driven. She sighed and melted against him, overwhelmed by the ambrosial flavor of his kiss—by his beguiling essence.

"I...I shouldn't let...I shouldn't kiss you. I..." she breathed when his mouth separated from hers a moment.

"I shouldn't ask you to," he argued.

"You didn't," she said.

"Do you want me to?" he asked. "Do you want me to ask your permission each time before I—"

"No!" she breathed, thrilling as he did not wait for the word to entirely leave her mouth before silencing her with his again.

He bound her in his arms as they kissed, pulling her tightly against the strong contours of his body. Ember felt the tear in her heart begin to hurt—the tear left there by Selkirk. Yet she did not wish to end her delicious exchange with Ridge. Her desire to kiss him—to be kissed by him—began to triumph over her fear. She would kiss him now, savor the feel of being in his arms, marvel at the masterful manner of his kiss. Her heart could ache later. Later she would worry; later she would face her fear. But for now, all she wanted was the sense of his lips blending with her own; all she wanted was to bathe in the bliss of the passion he rained over her— evoked in her.

She trembled—shuddered with delight—wondered if he noticed. He must have, and it disappointed her, for he broke from her then, brushing a strand of hair from her face.

"I should've bought the entire contents of that old sea dog's satchel," he mumbled, smiling.

Ember bit her lip, blushed, and stepped back out of his arms. "It's a beautiful bracelet," she said, studying the adornment at her wrist.

"Apparently," Ridge said.

She looked up to see him smiling at her. He winked, and her heart leapt.

"You must think I'm...that I'm..." she stammered, thinking of Esmeralda, the loose woman at the drinking establishment in town.

"I think I'm a cad," he interrupted, "and you probably should slap me next time."

Ember smiled—delighted that he'd said *next time.*

"I'll try," she told him.

"Come on," he said, taking her elbow and turning her toward the cottage, "before your mother thinks I'm up to no good."

She wanted to ask him. Ember wanted to ask him why he'd kissed her again. She wanted to hear him say that he was fond of her in the least of it—though she knew that he was. Most likely he only felt he owed her an insurmountable load of debt for finding him on the shore. But she wanted to pretend it was more, that he liked her because she was worth being liked. And what he must think! She was so willing to kiss him—a stranger! Yet he did not seem disgusted by her—quite the opposite.

"Does Lily have any suitors?" he asked.

Ember's heart cried out! Surely he did not mean to ask her for the sake of wanting the position himself. Still, the memory of Selkirk washed over her like some terrible disease.

"N-no," she answered plainly. "Wh-why do you ask?"

He shrugged. "I don't know. And what about you?" He smiled at her and added, "Though I suppose I should've asked you that before I used my siren's song on you yesterday...and just a moment ago."

She smiled, somewhat relieved. "No," she said. "No dashing swains are hiding in wait of Lily. And I...I prefer...I prefer..." She could not say what she meant. Fear of rejection was too thick in her.

"You prefer mermen," he chuckled.

Ember smiled and giggled. "You're a terrible tease," she told him. "One day I'll find something to tease you about, and then you'll be sorry for teasing me so."

"You can tease me any way and any time the notion comes over you, Ember Taffee."

Ember bit her lip, delighted. She blushed and glanced to the lovely bracelet at her wrist.

Lily gazed out the window, watching as Ember and Ridge neared the cottage. "Do you think he'll break her heart, Mother?" Lily asked. "Surely he wasn't sent for that purpose...do you think?"

Tempest smiled, though she knew the pain in her eldest daughter's heart. "I pray not," Tempest said, "though it may be her fear and trepidation may break his."

"I would never break his heart," Lily mumbled. "But he wasn't meant for me, was he?"

"Lily, darling," Tempest began, the sting of painful empathy for her daughter causing tears to fill her eyes.

"Do you think we can trust him with Ember, Mother?" she asked, changing the venue of their conversation slightly. "Do you think he would endeavor to seduce her?"

Tempest felt as if the very blood had drained from her body. A cold—a sickening, bitter ice—spread through her like an illness. Pushing her own fears to the corners of her mind, she said, "Endeavor he may. But Ember would not bow to it."

"But Ridge...he is so very handsome, after all. And Ember, if she loves him, she will love him with a pure desperation I cannot begin to fathom," Lily added.

"He will not seduce her to anything that would threaten her virtue," Tempest said, though her hands had begun to tremble.

"You seem to have a great deal of faith in a man we hardly know," Lily said.

Tempest forced a smile. "I have faith in Ember, Lily."

Lily smiled, somewhat soothed, and Tempest determined what she must do. In that instant she knew. She did own faith in her daughter, yet she knew how Ember would love Ridge if she allowed herself to love him. Ember would love him desperately. Tempest knew that desperate love was dangerous—perhaps the greatest and most wonderful love that existed but dangerous. Desperate love could weaken even the strongest character and resolve.

She would talk to him. It was time. Tempest determined that she would tell Ridge of Ember's manner of loving—a manner she'd inherited from her mother, a manner in which Tempest Taffee had loved not once but twice.

CHAPTER FIVE
THE WEATHERING OF A TEMPEST

Ridge was tired. He'd slept very little, if at all, for the past several nights and had worked hard the past several days. He was glad the merchant had closed his doors early, glad for the unexpected reprieve. He leaned back in the shore chair, covering his mouth as he yawned.

Tempest smiled at him from her seat in her own chair.

"Tired, darling?" she asked.

He nodded.

"Well, I don't doubt it. The cottage is comfortable...unless one is forced into sleeping on the floor. I'll rest easier knowing you have a comfortable bed at the inn." She looked at him, her smile broadening. "Though we will miss having you with us here," she added.

"And I'll miss being here," Ridge said. "What man would want to give up such an existence as lingering in isolation with three such beautiful women?"

Tempest laughed, her emerald eyes glistening with mirth. "Oh, you *are* a charmer, my darling. Perhaps Ember is right after all. Perhaps you are a son of Neptune, blessed with the siren's song of the merfolk."

Ridge chuckled and shook his head. "Unfortunately, I'm simply a man."

"Oh, I'm not so certain," Tempest teased. She patted his knee affectionately.

Ridge's heart knew disappointment in that moment. His room at the inn was ready. He'd be residing in town from now on. This would be his first night there, away from Taffee Cottage, and though he did not want to leave, he knew it was the best course.

Tempest had insisted he join them each evening for supper, however. She'd insisted on making certain he was well fed for at least one meal a day—or so she'd said. Ridge was sorely grateful for the invitation, for he'd begun to realize he could not endure a day that did not have the sight of Ember in it.

He returned his attention to the shore, to the place where Ember and Lily knelt, sifting through sand and gazing into tide pools in search of treasure.

"Perhaps they'll find the elusive angel wings Ember is so determined to discover," he said. "She says it's very hard to find two...two that are the remains of the same creature."

Tempest nodded. "Indeed. It is very difficult to find a set. The clam that they come from is very strong and buries itself very deep. I've only found a complete set three or four times in the last ten years...and all of them after a storm had been at sea." Tempest sighed. "But I daresay, with as many mermaid tears as Ember seems to find, she's bound to find a set of angel wing shells eventually. Anyway, it's the sea glass she loves most." Tempest paused, glancing to Ridge. "I think she loves them because of her father."

Ridge smiled. "Yes. She told me that it was her father who used to tell her the tales of the merfolk."

Tempest nodded. "My husband loved the sea," she whispered. Ridge's eyes narrowed as he looked at her—studied her dreamy, sad expression. "Each evening, whenever he was ashore, he'd take the girls here, sometimes build a small fire, spread a blanket on the sand and tell them tales of mermaids, of Neptune, of the creatures in the sea. He loved them so much...both of them."

Ridge felt a slight frown pucker his brow. He thought her assurance that Mariner Taffee loved both his daughters rather strange. "I'm certain that he did," he said. "How could any man not love both of them?"

Tempest looked at him, her expression rather daring, or mischievous—he couldn't tell which. "Well, you seem to have attached yourself more firmly to Ember," she stated, almost accusingly.

Ridge felt his cheeks warm a bit. "Yes. But a father...a father would easily care for both his daughters, equally care for them." He paused, considering his own father—of his father's favoritism toward himself. His father had ever made it perfectly clear that he favored his eldest son—that Daisy and Artie were not so favored as Ridge was. Thus, he added, "A good father would love them equally anyway."

"Oh, I promise you, Ridge, Mariner Taffee was a great father," she said. She turned her attention back to her daughters, who were now standing, studying something in the palm of Lily's hand. "He was a wonderful father, a magnificent lover, and a very forgiving, humble, and loving husband. Mariner did not place judgment on others the way most people do. Mariner understood tribulation, weakness, sin, and atonement."

Something in her tone—the sensitive emotion in her voice—caused him to look to her once more. He felt an odd impression wash over him, an almost ominous anticipation.

She looked to him then, smiling, her emerald eyes flashing with some unnamed, expressive passion. "I'd like to tell you my story, Ridge," Tempest said, "if you'll have it...if you'll protect it."

Ridge's eyes narrowed. He studied her for a moment, sensing that the story she wished to tell him was more than merely interesting but also deeply poignant. He was struck by the seemingly conflicting points in her countenance then—as if serenity fought to rein in some sort of wild nature. In this way, as in many others, Tempest looked more like Ember than she did Lily. Her eyes were bright and green as jewels, like Lily's. Yet her soft brown hair, delightful smile, and freckled button of a nose put him so in mind of Ember—and he was somehow glad.

"I'm always trustworthy for keeping a good story safe," Ridge said.

Still, he thought the light in Tempest's bright eyes dulled a little as she said, "I didn't say it was a good story."

Ridge sensed something momentous shimmering between them—likewise felt her trepidation, her fear. The protective nature in him owned the need to soothe her suddenly, and he said, "You're a strong woman, with two beautiful and very strong daughters. Hills and valleys—whichever or both—yours must be a good story. With such an outcome as you three Taffee beauties, how could it be otherwise?"

Tempest smiled, her green eyes brightening. "Oh, Ridge," she giggled, shaking her head. "I pity the women that have fallen in your wake, for you are too charming to be all good." She looked to the shore—to where Ember and Lily knelt once more in collecting sea treasure. "Still, what woman wants a man who is all good, say I? I am certain I do not…did not."

"Ah," Ridge said as understanding was his. "Am I to believe that there is a bad man at the center of this story you aim to tell me?"

Tempest looked back to him, still smiling. "Perhaps."

She swallowed and gazed out to sea for a time. Ridge waited—outwardly patient, inwardly eager.

"I've chosen to tell you my story, Ridge—chosen to tell you of things that my own daughters do not know the full measure of," she stated. "Are you wondering why I have chosen to confide such things in you?"

"I have an idea," Ridge mumbled, glancing away from her a moment. And he did. He knew Tempest was concerned for her daughters, namely Ember. He had acquaintances whose sole purpose in their pampered, arrogant lives was the seducing of women—specifically beautiful young women of innocent character. *Conquests*, they called them. These wealthy young men of privilege had no code of honor or chivalry, little or no concern for the consequences that befell their victims. "You're worried for your daughter's virtue," he mumbled. He was angry, but not at Tempest. He was angry that his appearance and supposed charm led near everyone he met to think him some predator of virtue—some slayer of purity.

"No," Tempest said. "I'm worried for her heart."

Ridge looked at her, amused suddenly. "You're lying," he said, grinning.

Tempest laughed, her eyes twinkling. "Perhaps...a little," she confessed. "I was young," she began then, "just three years younger than Ember is now. His name was Seward Conner, and he was first mate on one of my father's ships." She paused, inhaling a breath of what seemed to be courage. Her smile slowly faded, and she continued, "Oh, he was handsome! And ever so charming...Seward Conner." She paused and glanced to Ridge. "And not near so handsome and charming as you, my darling."

Ridge glanced away a moment, uncomfortable under Tempest's knowing gaze. The lovely, kind, and no doubt life-weathered woman knew the power a handsome and charming man could have on a young girl's heart. He sensed she knew it from her own experience. He knew it too, from his own experience as well, though he'd never endeavored to misuse the power. An odd and unwelcome understanding was washing over him. He wondered whether Tempest Taffee had the power to read his mind—or to place her own thoughts into his.

"Yes, Seward was charming, and I fell in love with him," she sighed. "Desperately in love—for that is how I love, Ridge...desperately. That is how one of my daughters loves as well. Can you guess which one?"

Ridge nodded, dared to look at her, and was relieved when he found her smiling at him with trust and understanding. "I can," he answered.

Tempest nodded and returned her gaze to the sea. "I thought I might die if Seward did not love me in return," she said. "I truly thought I might die. And I was so young, my heart so truly in the hands of another." She paused, her smile fading again as a shadow seemed to pass over her lovely, Ember-like face. "I will not dwell on particulars, Ridge. Let it simply be said that I was young and Seward was charming...and that I loved him with such a wild desperation as to think I could not go on living if I did not own his heart." She shook her head—closed her eyes a moment. "He promised his love to me...told me I owned his heart as no other woman ever would. He went to my father and begged for my hand in marriage, but Father was furious and refused. My father did not see the benefit in allowing his daughter to wed a simple sailor—a sailor with no money, no ship of his own to command, and little or no prospect of ever rising to recognition of any kind. I begged my father not to dismiss Seward from his rank as first mate, and he agreed. Father did not dismiss Seward, but he did set him as first mate on a ship bound for the east. Seward was to be gone for months, perhaps more than a year, and I was heartbroken. We met one last time, the night before he was meant to set sail. We met near the Dirk and the Mermaid— Mermaid Rock, the large rock formation in the cove. Do you know it?" She looked to Ridge, her eyes moist.

Ridge shook his head. "No," he mumbled.

Tempest's pretty lips curved into a slight smile. "You must see it. It is quite lovely, and there is such a legend surrounding it." She inhaled a long breath and breathed a heavy sigh. Looking again toward the tender waves gently breaking onto the sand, she said, "We met, Seward and I, one last time...met as lovers about to be stripped of one another's company for we knew not how long. Our rendezvous, our secret tryst...I do not know what weakened me— whether it was overpowering love, desperation, despair, or all of them stirred together. Yet I was weak in that last hour of my last night with my lover." She looked to Ridge once more and asked, "Can you guess the consequence of my weak, desperate love?"

Ridge felt his face grow uncomfortably hot. He was not at ease in sitting with a woman in discussion of such things. Remembering Tempest's remarks about Mariner Taffee loving both his daughters, he nodded toward Tempest's daughters and managed to answer, "From your implications...I would guess that perhaps the lovely Lily there on the shore was the consequence."

Tempest smiled and nodded. "Yes," she affirmed. "I was weak— far weaker than I should have been, even for such a tender age," she said. Again she paused, inhaling a deep breath and exhaling a sigh.

Ridge knew it was difficult for Tempest to relate the history to him. Also, he suspected her reason for telling it to him, and he was admittedly offended. She did suspect him of being a seducer.

"Tempest, I would never—" he began.

"I know, my darling," she said, placing a reassuring hand on his knee. "I know you think you would never lead a woman into…but you mistake my reason for telling you my story, a story which is far from its end." She paused, tenderly smiling at him. "I am a soul-reader, Ridge," she said. "I would not have let you linger with us if I had not read yours to be without selfish, rapacious intent."

Somewhat relieved that Tempest was not telling him her history in order to warn him against seducing Ember, he nodded, determined to hold his tongue and allow her to continue.

"Seward sailed the next morning. The ship was lost within the week. Her crew went with her to the bottom of the sea—all her crew. My Seward was drowned," Tempest explained.

Ridge frowned. He had not expected such a quick and tragic end for Seward.

"Soon it became known to me…soon I understood that Lily was there, that I was to have a baby," Tempest whispered. Ridge had to strain his hearing to hear her over the waves and gulls. "I went first to my mother, and it was she who told my father. Oddly, he did not shout at me nor lay a hand of harm to me. Simply he married me to Nicholas Alexander, an ancient yet very wealthy merchant who had been his friend for many years. Nicholas Alexander had previously attempted to convince my father to allow him to take me to wife. I was sixteen. Nicholas was then fifty-seven."

"Fifty-seven?" Ridge exclaimed, looking to Tempest with near nausea.

Tempest smiled, seeming amused at his horror. "Did I deserve any better than to be wed to an old man?"

"Yes!" Ridge growled. "Fifty-seven?" He shook his head, disgusted at the thought of an old man owning such a young girl as wife.

Tempest placed a tender hand to Ridge's cheek. "I thank you for that, Ridge. I have always thought I deserved such a trial as I found in knowing Nicholas as my husband for three years. You have eased my heart a little."

"Fifty-seven," Ridge growled, frowning at her.

Tempest giggled, sighed, and continued. "Nicholas never knew Lily was not his daughter. I saw no reason to hurt him. I did not love him, for he was cruel and brutal to me. Yet he did not deserve the manipulation my father had exacted. And after all, he did provide for Lily and me. Thus, it was simply assumed Lily had been born before her time. She was very small when she was birthed."

"Does Lily know?" Ridge could not keep from asking. "Does she know Seward Conner is her father and not the old man you did not love?"

"No," Tempest said. "She thinks Nicholas was her true father. Many times I have agonized over whether she should be told the truth. But I cannot bring myself to tell her…to tell her that I was once a weak-minded, weak-willed girl. Still, Nicholas did not love her, and even as young as she was, she knew she was not loved by him. It haunts her; I know it does. Mariner loved her as his own, of course. My Mariner, he knew the truth, yet he loved her the same as he did Ember."

Ridge frowned. He was not so certain that Lily would not be happier in knowing she had been conceived in love—however errant the circumstances—rather than having been sired by a cruel, brutal old man. Still, he said nothing, for it was not his place.

"Nicholas died when Lily was three," Tempest continued, "and I was glad of it." She shook her head, closed her eyes, and winced. "That was my second great sin—finding relief in the death of the man who had provided for me and the child he had not fathered." She opened her eyes once more, still looking out over the waves. "But I am repentant and will not linger on my sins," she whispered.

She drew a deep breath. "When Nicholas died, he left his estate—his ships and the bulk of his wealth—to a mistress," she said.

"What?" Ridge exclaimed.

"It is true," she affirmed. "I often wondered if he knew about Lily. But I think not. I think he simply cared for his mistress more than he did Lily and I...and rightly so, I suppose. He left us the cottage and the acreage around it, here along the shore," she said, nodding toward the sea. "Enough allowance to carry us through...if only barely. Still, he did not forsake us altogether, and for that I am thankful, for I did not deserve even that good treatment."

"I would argue that—" Ridge began.

Tempest's tender hand on his knee silenced him once more, however. "Nicholas died, and I would not go back to my father's house. So Lily and I moved to the cottage, and we were happy," she continued. "I felt free of my sins in a manner...or at least free to suffer the knowledge of them in solitude. And, oh, how I loved my little girl! My little Lily, who grew more and more to look like her father with each passing day. I was welcomed in town, for people felt sorry for me in my husband having been so cruel to his wife and daughter in the end. No one knew the truth, so I was accepted. Life went along. Lily and I were happy here. Yet as I told you, when I love, I love with a desperation that is unmatched, and it was there— just where Lily and Ember linger in searching for treasure—that I met the love who would own me even more fully than had Seward."

Ridge looked to where Ember and Lily again stood studying something in Lily's hand.

"It was there I met Captain Mariner Taffee," she said.

Ridge smiled as he saw the light return to Tempest's eyes. He could well see the love she still carried for him.

"I was walking—Lily and I were walking one morning," Tempest began, "just there, just where the girls are now. We were combing the shore for treasure." She smiled. "I remember Lily found a lovely shell. Mariner came upon us, and I knew at once his soul was good...and safe." She exhaled a light laughter. "He told Lily a mermaid had dropped the shell, that there had been a full moon the night before, that mermaids can come ashore when the moon is full. He told Lily he was certain the shell had fallen from a mermaid's necklace." She looked to Ridge, her smile broadening. "Lily was charmed, of course…and so was I."

Ridge smiled, though he could not quite discern whether he felt joy or pain. "And you loved him…desperately," he said in a low voice.

"Desperately!" Tempest breathed, again gazing out to sea. "Oh, so very desperately—far more desperately even than I had loved Seward." She paused a moment. "We married only three weeks after our first meeting, and Ember was born within a year." She looked to him. "I know you see me in her," she told him, "but she is ever so much more her father, and not just for the sake of her midnight eyes. Her spirit is so like his—her strength, her love of the sea."

Ridge sighed. "She loves the sea, though it took her father from her."

"Pirates took her father from her," Tempest said.

"Pirates?" Ridge asked.

"Yes," Tempest answered. "Oh, piracy is rare these days, but it still exists. Mariner was captain of a ship, a ship that was set upon by pirates. His ship was eventually recovered some years later, and the tale was told by the surviving pirates of how they had forced all hands overboard when they'd taken the ship…forced them into the sea." She shook her head and breathed a sad laugh. "Sometimes I dream—I dream that Mariner and Seward are both there, at the bottom of the sea, that the fathers of my two girls are friends, that they talk of us and miss us, and I wake feeling sinful and guilty once more—for the moment I met Mariner, I never missed Seward again."

Ridge sighed, his heart feeling heavy and sore. He thought of Tempest, a young girl looking much as Ember did now—thought of her pain, of her desperation in loving Seward. He thought of the horrible realization that must have overwhelmed her when she realized she'd fallen prey to weakness in the arms of Seward. He thought of her father—a cruel, heartless man—and he measured him against his own father, thinking they would have made good bedfellows. His stomach churned at the thought of the poor young girl Tempest, already carrying the weight of sin and guilt, forced to marry a man forty years her senior—pressed to keep the secret of Lily's true sire.

He looked to Tempest, and his eyes narrowed.

"What are you thinking, handsome castaway?" Tempest asked. Though she smiled, he saw the fear in her eyes. "Are you thinking that I should be stoned for my sins? That I—"

"I'm thinking that you are a stronger woman than even I surmised, Tempest Taffee," he interrupted. "To have endured such tragic experiences...such loss. Yet to own two such beautiful daughters, to have loved and been loved so desperately. Your wisdom was gained by near insurmountable and, no doubt, haunting means. Yet here you are, a beautiful, virtuous woman, with two beautiful and virtuous daughters." He looked back to the shore, adding, "If you think I'm sitting in judgment of you, then you're wrong." Ridge paused a moment. "My grandmother always said that if a person wished to know thick misery, to experience the trials that might well kill him—if a man or woman longs to endure hardship, heartache, loss, and wretchedness, then let them simply sit in the unrighteous, arrogant judgment of others. Arrogance is the sure path to tribulation and woeful sorrow." He looked to her. "Mistakes scar us—our hearts and our bodies, yes, but more often our souls. Still, we can choose to learn from our sins and transgressions and—in our humble, repentant state—offer guidance to others, guidance that may help to avoid owning pain...or causing it. Perhaps our experience may heal the scars others carry or prevent them altogether."

Tempest's eyes narrowed as she studied him. Ridge did not avoid her gaze; rather he met it with confidence. He did not say the things he had said because he thought it was what she wanted to hear; he had said them because they were the feelings of his heart, the true opinions of his soul. He was not perfect—no, indeed not! Then who was he to think ill of her for a moment of weakness, the price for which she paid with a suffering of the soul he could not imagine?

"You think I've told you my story because I'm fearful you will seduce my daughter," she stated.

"I think there are many reasons you told it to me," he admitted, "and I've no doubt there are some I don't yet consciously comprehend. But, yes, I think you're worried for Ember. I think you've sensed my...my strong attraction to her, and it concerns you. You would not be a good mother if it didn't."

Tempest's eyes narrowed again. "You spoke of scars...of scars of the heart and soul," she said.

"Yes," he confirmed. "We, all of us, carry scars...of one sort or the other."

"What if I told you my story not because I fear you may falter and press Ember to weakness but because Ember herself owns scars—scars that haunt her, scars that yet pain her? What then?"

Ridge was caught by surprise. What was she saying? Was she trying to tell him that her daughter had suffered a similar weakness as she once had? Was she thinking his attraction to Ember would waver if she were not so unscathed as she seemed?

"Ember is not as weak as her mother once was," she said. "But her heart is pure and tender. She loves pure as desperately as I."

Her gaze was so intense as to cause him to feel she could read his thoughts—his very soul. He remembered then that she was a determiner of souls, and he knew she was determining his. Ridge understood then. "You're afraid I'll break her heart," he mumbled.

When Tempest did not respond, an uncomfortable sense of responsibility was his sudden companion. To break Ember's heart—to be the cause of making her unhappy—it literally sickened him. Yet could he break her heart? In order to break her heart, she would have to love him, and she couldn't possibly love him. Still, he knew she was attracted to him, and this gave him reason to feel a sense of accountability.

"I confess...I confess to owning a near obsessive attraction to her," he mumbled. "I'll confess to you also that I have kissed her, on two occasions, and not the way some lily-scented schoolboy might kiss a girl...but the way a man kisses a woman with wanton desire."

"Did she kiss you back?" she asked.

Ridge looked up, astonished that this should be her response to his confessions. "Uh…yes," he stammered.

"Do you love her?" she blatantly asked.

"Well, I certainly love to kiss her," he admitted with all honesty.

He was startled as Tempest laughed then, tossing wavy brown curls to cascade over her back. "And I'm certain that you do, Ridge," she sighed. "But do you love her? Do you love my Ember?"

"How can I?" he asked. "I've not known her half the month. How can I love her? How can she love me? We're still strangers."

He'd said it—implied that it would be impossible to know if he loved Ember after so short an acquaintance. And yet his heart—his heart that swelled to an almost painful crescendo whenever he thought of Ember—was in exorbitant opposition with his words.

Tempest, still smiling, eyes bright with an emerald shine, leaned toward him. "Every love begins with two strangers, Ridge darling," she told him. "Every love begins that way."

Her eyes misted, and Ridge thought she looked so like Ember in that moment.

"I only ask that should you become aware that you do not love her, you have the compassion to set her free…before you've crushed her," she whispered. "I fear her heart could not survive the scars you would inflict."

"And what of me?" he asked. "What if I'm the one whose heart is to bear the wound?"

Tempest smiled. "I know my daughter," she said. "Your heart is already safe, darling."

Ridge felt his body inhale something akin to a gasp. Was she telling him he already owned Ember's heart? He could not believe it. He would not—not yet.

"I can see I've laden too much upon you, Ridge," she said, sighing as if she'd just endured some great physical exertion. "I've said all my heart felt pressed to." She smiled at him. "As you said, I would not be a good mother if I hadn't."

He chuckled and looked up when he heard Lily and Ember squeal. Both girls squealed again, and Lily tossed a shell to the sand as they danced about as if something had suddenly taken to crawling over their flesh.

Tempest giggled. "It seems they found something that wasn't ready to be put in a bottle on the mantel."

Ridge laughed as Ember squealed and tossed something to the sand as well.

"I'm glad she didn't scream and toss me back," he said.

Tempest laughed, her countenance filled only with mirth.

Still, something had been eating at Ridge's mind, and he felt impressed to address it, though he feared the consequences may not be pleasant. "May I say something, something that may offend you, though my intention is only to better the life of your daughter?" he asked.

"Of course, if you think it will benefit Ember," she agreed.

Ridge inhaled a deep breath of courage, glancing again to the two young women on the shore.

"Not Ember, Tempest...but Lily."

"Lily?" Tempest asked. He could see the curiosity in her expression.

He nodded and began, "When I spoke of our experiences in life—that our mistakes and what we learn from them might benefit others—I think too experiences we endure that are not borne from our own mistakes but simply borne of experience itself...I think that too may benefit others."

Tempest was quiet a moment—pensive. She studied him, and he could nearly feel her again determining his soul. "You own experience that you think might benefit Lily?" she asked.

He nodded and swallowed the lump of trepidation in his throat, for he did not want to offend or hurt the mother of the woman he...loved to kiss. "I think perhaps...I think perhaps it would benefit Lily to know the truth, to know her father was a young sailor named Seward Conner, who loved her mother so madly as to be driven to reckless abandon. I think she should know it was he who was her father and not the hardhearted, moth-eaten old merchant Nicholas

Alexander, who loved his mistress more than his own family," he said.

Tempest looked away a moment. "I...I have often wondered if she should be told. She struggles with feeling of worth. Ember is so lighthearted and vibrant...or so she appears. Ember is so like her father, and I know Lily is envious of her, though she tries not to be, for the sake of loving her so thoroughly. I know she worries that she is not like Mariner...or me, for that matter. In truth, she is her father's image. She owns the exact color of his hair—that dark, ebony, beautiful hair—and she has his demeanor as well, and his gift for drawing and painting. Seward was a masterful artist." She paused and looked at him, and he saw the fear and worry in her eyes. "But what if the knowledge...what if the truth only serves to damage her self-worth? The self-worth that her father...her true father...the self-worth Mariner and I worked so desperately to nurture in her? What if her mother's sin...my lies—"

"My father doesn't love me, Tempest," Ridge interrupted. He shrugged. "Oh, he loves me for inheriting my mother's...'your mother's beauty that will bewitch and manipulate the world into granting you anything you want,' as he puts it. He sees the potential power my skills and natural wit can offer, but he doesn't love me, and he never loved my mother for anything other than her beauty." He looked at her, his eyes narrowing. "To know I had been conceived in love—in love, instead of as the result of an arranged marriage, a marriage my mother had no choice but to accept, a marriage arranged for the sake of money and position—it would comfort me, Tempest." He shook his head, his emotions closer to the surface than he would have preferred. "I cannot think of her having to endure his attentions. It sickens me." He looked to Tempest. He'd never seen her frown before. "You would not be encouraging her toward immorality by telling her the truth, Tempest," he said. "The truth will set her free. I think the truth will free her."

Tempest swallowed and brushed a tear from one cheek. "Mariner...he and I...we used to talk about it," she whispered. "If he hadn't have died, his love would've completed her, and she might not struggle as she does now. And still…still he thought she should know. He wanted her to know the truth, just as he wanted her to know that it didn't matter to him who had fathered her first, because he loved her. She was his. He was her father, and she was his Lily."

"I have no right to even suggest this to you, Tempest," Ridge said. His heart was beating madly for fear he would offend the mother of the woman he…the woman he loved to kiss—for fear she might tell him never to return to the cottage. "But…but I would have loved to have had a father who loved my mother, to know that I was the result of love instead of the result of political trade for gain."

She was quiet for a long moment. Then she looked at him and smiled. "Mariner would agree with you," she whispered.

A rather uncomfortable sensation traveled through Ridge. "Would your Mariner…would Ember's father have approved of me? Of my…of my loving to kiss his youngest daughter?" he ventured.

Tempest giggled. "Yes! Yes, he would have."

Ridge sighed with relief and smiled. "Very well then," he said. He stood up, pulled his shirt off over his head with one swift motion, and tossed it onto the chair. "Lily!" he called, still looking at Tempest. "Your mother wants to speak with you."

"Oh, Ridge, no! Not now! Not yet!" Tempest gasped.

"She will be the happier for it in the end, Tempest," he told her.

Ember brushed the hair back from her face as she turned to see Ridge striding toward her. As was the case each time she saw him, her heart began to hammer with near exhausting excitement.

"Here," Lily said, taking the cluster of tiny shells from Ember's hand. "Let me take them." Lily smiled, whispering, "I think your pretty merman would rather your hands were free to caress his broad merman's chest."

"Lily!" Ember scolded in a whisper.

But Lily only giggled, turned, and started toward the place where their mother sat.

"Walk with me, Ember," Ridge said, taking her hand and fairly pulling her along with him—and in the opposite direction of her mother and Lily.

Though Ember loved the feel of his hand holding tight to hers—though the thought of being alone with him caused her stomach to quiver with near overwhelming delight—she sensed he was not so composed as he was attempting to appear.

"Stop," she said, surprised when he obeyed her command.

He turned, looking at her, the slightest of frowns on his broad, handsome brow.

Ember inhaled a calming breath and searched the blue pools of his eyes. She was her mother's daughter, and she too could determine a soul.

"You talked to my mother for a long time," she said.

"Yes," he said. "She wanted to make sure I had...honorable intentions toward you."

"And do you?" she asked, still studying his countenance.

He grinned. "Mostly," he said, bending down to quickly taste her mouth.

Ember giggled, delighted by his flirting. There was no trace of dishonesty in his eyes—only mischief and desire. She bit her lower lip, wishing he would kiss her again.

"And you're wanting to walk with me?" she asked him.

"Yes," he said. "To walk with you...to hear your voice."

"Hear my voice?" she giggled.

"Yes," he affirmed. "Tell me about your father, Ember. Tell me about Mariner Taffee."

Ember simultaneously smiled and frowned. "My father? Why?"

"Because he sounds like a good man...a great man...a man it would benefit others to emulate."

Ember sighed as melancholy and joy mingled in her bosom. "So that's what you and Mother were talking about so long," she said. "Captain Mariner Taffee...my father. It's why she never remarried. No man can touch her heart, for even in heaven, he holds it tightly to him."

Ridge smiled. Ember's dark eyes were glistening with love, adoration, for a good and loving father. Oh, it was true he wanted to simply take her in his arms and kiss her until they both melted into oblivion, but his conversation with Tempest had awakened his mind toward something else. He was attracted to Ember, as he'd never been attracted to a woman before; this fact was infallible. She was attracted to him—the proof in the passion evoked in her when they kissed. Still, there was more to love than physical passion. There was emotional fervor, a fusing of souls. Ridge wanted to know Ember, everything about her—her opinions, her musings, her favoritisms. He wanted to be certain it was Ember Taffee he loved and not just her Venus allure. Furthermore, he wanted evidence that her mother was right—that his heart was already safe. Tempest had implied that Ember loved him, and Ridge wanted proof. Could such a wild, playful beauty truly love him?

Every love begins with two strangers, Ember's mother had said.

Her assurance was simplistic—and utterly profound. It was true. Every love did begin with two strangers. Then if this were the beginning of love, the next step would be for two strangers to come to know one another. Thus, he would know Ember—ensure that she knew him—for then and only then could two strangers become lovers.

Ember smiled as Ridge tightened his grip on her hand. The muscles in his arms were firm and warm, and she pressed her own arm against his as they walked.

"Tell me, then," he said. "Tell me about Mariner Taffee."
Ember sighed and smiled as he began to lead her along the shore at a leisurely, meandering pace.

"He was captain of the Minerva Diana," Ember began, "and his eyes were the same as mine."

"Mmm," he mumbled. "So Captain Mariner Taffee had eyes forged of onyx and diamonds, dark and clear as the midnight skies, with the light of a million stars glistening in them?" he asked.

Ember giggled, delighted by his flattery.

"Tell me more, Ember Taffee," he said, smiling. "For I'm determined to know your father…through you."

"Very well, Ridge West," she said. "I will tell you of Captain Mariner Taffee, of Captain Taffee and his one true love."

"The sea?" Ridge asked.

Ember shook her head and felt the familiar warmth of tears bright in her eyes. "No. My mother."

CHAPTER SIX

THE HARROWED HEIR

"And she loves him as much in this very minute as she did before the sea took him," Ember sighed. "Fourteen years he's been gone." She smiled, shaking her head in awed admiration. "And my mother's love for my father has never lessened...not a wink."

"And yet she must've been very young when he was lost," Ridge offered.

"Mother received the news of my father's being lost at sea two days before her twenty-sixth birthday," Ember explained, her heart aching for her mother's years of mourning her father, of missing her lover with every drawn breath. "As much as I love to find the treasures the sea sprinkles on the shore, to listen to the gulls and the surf, sometimes I hate the sea for taking him from us. Father always told me Neptune is a fickle creature, that the mythical gods of Rome toy with human hearts to intrigue and entertain themselves at our expense."

Ember gazed up at Ridge—studied him as he stared out over the water. She fancied Neptune was in a benevolent mood of recent. There hadn't been a storm in weeks, not since just before he'd washed Ridge ashore. Was Neptune feeling giddy? Had he kept the storms at bay for the comfort of those who lived near the sea? Had he washed Adonis ashore in the form of Ridge West, simply to delight Ember, to try to compensate for the wound he'd inflicted when he'd allowed his realm of the sea to take her father?

"And no man ever tried to heal your mother's heart?" Ridge asked.

Ember shrugged. "There have been men who have wanted to try…good men. One in particular, a solicitor in town, Ivan Derrickson. Mother liked Ivan well enough. She's known him for years, since she was widowed." Ember thought aloud then, "Did you know she was widowed? That she had been married once before my father?"

Ridge nodded. "Yes," he said.

Ember sighed and continued, "Ivan Derrickson is a good man, but Mother's whole heart belongs to Father still, even now, for all eternity. Mother told Ivan that, though she was fond of him, counted him one of her greatest friends, it would not be right to marry him when she was not in love with him. Ivan would have been good to her, and he liked Lily and me, but Mother could not have loved him. She could not have endured his touch or…" Ember paused. A great sadness was overtaking her at having lingered so long in thinking of her father's loss and her mother's pain. Her own pain where her father was concerned was deep and aching, but it was the knowledge of her mother's pain that haunted her. "Do you feel you know him now?" she asked, stooping to pick up a pretty shell that was peeking from the sand.

"I do," Ridge said. "He was the greatest of men. It is obvious by the legacy of joy and love he left behind."

"Then come here," Ember said, taking his hand. She led him to a small rock and sat down. "It's your turn now." He sat down next to her, and she smiled. Glancing up to Mermaid Rock, she thought of the last time she'd been to the cove—of coming upon Lily reading her diary, of a conversation of merfolk with Ridge that led to his kissing her. Her bosom fluttered at the memory, her arms prickling with a delightful deluge of goose bumps.

"My turn?" he asked.

"Yes," Ember said. "I want to know something through you. I want to hear your voice. Goodness knows I've been rambling on and on. Your ears must be aching!"

He chuckled and brushed a strand of windblown hair from her cheek. "Your voice could never cause ears to ache, Ember," he said. "I swear I could listen to you for days on end and not grow weary."

Ember rolled her eyes. "What do you want?" she giggled. "You're in a flattering mood. You must want something."

His smile broadened, mischief gleaming in his mind. "Oh, I can't tell you what I want," he said. "Propriety would demand you flee from me as quickly as your feet could carry you."

Ember giggled. How she loved when he flirted with her, his delicious insinuations. "Very well, charmer, then tell me about your parents." A disturbing thought crossed her mind. She did not wish to cause him pain. "If…if you wish to. If they are still living or it is not too painful."

Ridge paused. He felt his own eyes narrow. His mouth watered as he studied her. He wanted to kiss her! In truth, he wanted to far more than kiss her, but he was a good man—a man of ethics and moral conduct. Furthermore, he cared too much for her to ever press her to anything beyond sharing impassioned kisses.

He cared for her. He did. In that moment, he knew that the time had come for full honesty. He would tell her the truth—risk her disapproval, perhaps her revulsion. Still, it must be done. If every love began with two strangers, then true love could not flourish safely without truth. He would risk it—for Ember Taffee was worth the risk.

Ember watched as Ridge inhaled a deep breath. He exhaled slowly, glancing away from her and out to sea once more.

"What if I come from a sordid history?" he asked.

"Are you sordid?" she asked in return.

"I…I don't think so," he chuckled.

Ember shrugged and smiled at him. "Then tell me your sordid history, Ridge West. It can't be so bad if you were its result."

He smiled at her, but she noted the sadness, the shadow of apprehension in his eyes.

"As your father was a good, loving, strong, and kind man—a man to be admired and emulated—mine is Mariner Taffee's exact opposite," he began. "He negotiated for my mother, married her against her will when she was seventeen. She was very beautiful." He paused and looked to the sea. "Hair as black as pitch, as soft and as fragrant as heaven. Her eyes were blue…like mine." He paused, grinning slightly. "I have my mother's eyes, just as you have your father's."

Ember smiled, thrilling with delight as she remembered how he'd described her eyes—forged of onyx and diamonds, clear as the midnight sky glistening with stars.

"Then her eyes were sapphire?" she asked. "Far bluer than the sky, or even the sea, with the power to mesmerize with one glance?"

He chuckled, caressing her cheek with the back of one hand. "Well, that's how I saw her eyes, at least," he said. "Her name was Mirabella. It means—"

"She of incredible beauty," Ember interrupted.

He smiled and nodded. Ember thought it very befitting that Ridge's mother should be named for her incredible beauty. She fancied for a moment that in looking at him, she knew what his mother must look like—or looked like—for he was speaking of her in the past tense.

"And her beauty was not only of the flesh sort," he continued. "My mother was kind, loving, compassionate, as patient as Job and just as enduring."

"She…she was lost?" Ember ventured.

"When I was fifteen," he answered. "She was overtaken by a cough, one that could not be eased." He looked at her. "She was consumptive…and she died."

"I'm sorry," Ember whispered as a sharp pain of empathy resonated through her entire being. She nearly clutched at her heart, for it was completely thoroughgoing.

"My mother was my strength…the savior of my soul and integrity in many ways," he continued. "My father is a powerful man, Ember. He owns incredible political position, hordes wealth beyond imagination and he loves only power. He did not love me for more than that I was his 'beautiful son,' as he used to say. His hopes are still that I will follow his disposition and character, his thirst for power, his lust for…"

Ember felt her eyebrows arch in astonishment. How could it be that Ridge was sired by such a man?

"But I am my mother's son, not my father's," he continued, "and it sorely vexes him. He knew I would not emulate him, that I would be my own man, that he could not mold me to love power and money more than people. Thus, he married again, this time to a wealth-seeking woman…one who was just as heartless."

"Was?" Ember prodded. A stepmother—also lost?

"Yes," he affirmed. "Fiona, my stepmother. She died in childbirth, in bearing my half-brother and sister, Arthur and Daisy."

"Daisy?" Ember said, smiling. It seemed an odd name for a child born to expectation of social position.

Ridge chuckled. "Yes, Daisy. My father had signed Artie's birth certificate, naming him Arthur—after himself, of course. My mother begged him not to name me after himself, and somehow she won that battle, though I still cannot fathom how. But Fiona had died in delivering the twins, so there was no mother to speak for my brother Artie. But when the attending physician asked my father what Daisy's name was to be, he wanted her to be called Maude, after his mother. The physician asked my father what Daisy's name was to be so that he could certify it, and my father only mumbled, 'Maude.' The physician didn't hear him and turned to me, asking, 'What was that?'" Ridge chuckled again. "I told him my father had said her name was to be Daisy. It was my mother's middle name." He shrugged. "So the physician signed the certificate stating Daisy's name as such, and he left. My father never referred to Daisy as anything other than 'the girl child' for many, many, months, so he wasn't too furious when the day came that he called her Maude and I told him I had named her Daisy. He was rather indifferent about her, after all."

Ember shook her head, amused by Ridge's intervention on Daisy's behalf—saddened by the fact that Ridge's father was such a hardhearted man.

"How old are they?" she asked him. "Your brother and sister?"

"Six years," he said.

"Six years!" Ember exclaimed. "Why…why, they're only babies!"

Ridge nodded and frowned. "Yes," he mumbled. "They have a good governess now, but I worry when they are older…that my father's influence will begin to seep into their souls."

"Perhaps you could snatch them away from him," Ember suggested. Her heart feared for the two children that she didn't even know. Ridge's father sounded to be a terrible man! She hated to think of little Artie and Daisy in his possession.

Ridge smiled, nodding. "I have thought about it. Very often I have thought about it. My father would give up Daisy easily enough. He doesn't see any worth in her. But Artie…in Artie he sees the chance to have everything I am not—a son who will be molded to what he wants him to be." He sighed. "It's difficult to consider."

Ember's eyes narrowed as she looked at him. It was unusual for the son of such a man to want anything other than the wealth and position afforded him by his father. Furthermore, it was unusual that such a man should allow a son—an heir—to live apart from him, to work for a merchant—to work at all!

"How is it that you are away from him, Ridge?" she asked. "It seems he would—"

"Father attempted to teach me his ways, beginning when I was a very young boy," he began. "He taught me trade, investment, all manner of commerce and speculation. University taught me the rest, and all the while he would give me money—money that I would invest and trade. I was quite successful at multiplying what he gave me…and then making investments and purchases in my own name."

"So, with his money, the profits you earned…you made your own way?" she asked.

He nodded. "Though Father hoped I would have his mind for business, I think he always thought I was too much my mother's son to succeed at anything other than being admired for resembling her. He told me I could pocket any profit I made with the money he allotted me to dabble with…so long as I paid him the beginning sum. And so I did."

Ember frowned. "But…but you were working aboard a ship."

He nodded. "I made my own way, Ember, but it doesn't mean I am by any means as wealthy as my father or that I shouldn't continue to labor hard. Therefore, I work because it's what a man should do. It's what I want to do. In fact, it's why I left the merchant I was employed by—because he learned who my father was. He became fearful of me—rather, of my father's power—and I left. I found work aboard that ship, but they also discovered the name of my sire…and so determined to hold me for ransom."

Ember's eyes narrowed as she remembered what Ridge had told her and her mother and sister about how he'd come to be washed ashore near the cottage. He'd said the sailors on the ship had tried to force him to inflict cruelty on another.

"So you jumped ship before they could overwhelm you, before they could ransom you to your father?" she asked. "Would your father have paid the ransom?"

"Of course," he said, "for he would know it would cause me to feel indebted to him. In that, he would endeavor to control me." He paused. "Artie and Daisy, they are the other reason I must keep from my father. I know he would use them to manipulate me in some way, if he knew where I was. So to all the world I'm Ridge West, trade negotiator for the merchant Morgan." He smiled at her. "Yes, trade negotiator and merman, of course."

Ember giggled and could not resist reaching up to place her palm against his rugged jaw. "Is your name really Ridge?" she asked.

His eyes sparkled as he gazed at her. "Yes," he said, "though I confess my full name is Chamridge…Chamridge Westminster."

Ember gasped. She felt her eyes widen. "Westminster?" she exclaimed.

"Hush, my pretty mermaid," he said, covering her mouth with one hand, "lest someone hear you."

Ember's heart was pounding with sudden anxiety. This was Arthur Westminster's son? Arthur Westminster, the richest man on any eastern coast? Ember's heart began to ache with fear. It was inconceivable that such a man as Chamridge Westminster—heir to one of the greatest fortunes in the world—would ever find true interest in a simple girl from a seaside cottage.

Ridge could see the panic in her eyes—the fear and sudden heartache. It was part of what he'd feared—that she would think him a liar, unstable, an exaggerator of the truth of his principles. He stood, taking hold of her arms, raising her to her feet—though he would not let her run from him. He would make her believe the certainty of his true character.

"You're sitting in judgment of me, Ember," he nearly growled, frowning at her. His grip was tight at her arms, his eyes smoldering with determination. "But if you are to judge me, then I beg you to judge me by my mother in me and not merely for bearing the name of the monster who sired me."

Still, she trembled, afraid of her own feelings for him. She was falling in love with him! No! She was already in love with him! Even for the warnings of her heart, she loved him. It was true she was guarded, that she had not released her full heart to him, for it remembered too well the pain and scars Selkirk Beacon had left upon it. Yet how could she hope that the son of Arthur Westminster would linger with the simple daughter of a lost sea captain?

"I'm the same man I was before I told you the whole of it, Ember," he pleaded. "The same man who owns your mother's confidence, the same man who mourns the loss of your father with you. I'm the same man who claims to be a merman and tries to seduce you with a siren's song. I have in no way altered simply because I've told you more of my history. Please, Ember, you're looking at me as if I were some sort of villain!"

Ember tried to think—tried to find a calm, ordered thought. How could she tell him that it was not so much who his father was but rather that who he was might ensure he would hurt her? He would leave, wouldn't he? Hadn't he been forced to leave the employment of a merchant who discovered his true identity? Hadn't he jumped from a ship into a merciless sea to escape others who had discovered the same? What if the merchant Morgan determined Ridge was Arthur Westminster's son? Would Ridge be forced to leave?

"I'm not judging you," she whispered then. "I promise I'm not judging because of your father. And even if I were to judge you, how could I judge you harshly when it is obvious you are your mother's son and not your father's, when you have endeavored to make your own way, to live an honorable life?"

"Then what is the doubt and fear I see in your black eyes, Ember?" he asked. "I swear that the sparkle lingering in them a moment ago is lost in shadow now." His grip at her arms tightened. "I am no villain, Ember."

Ember placed a palm to his cheek. Near frantically he took the hand, pressing a kiss to her tender palm.

"I know that," she whispered. "I only…I only…what if someone here discovers who you are?"

He frowned. "I'm Ridge West, tradesman for the merchant Morgan."

She understood and scolded herself for causing him pain. "I mean, what if someone here discovers who your father is?" she asked.

He frowned, and she knew he did not understand her concern.

Ridge shrugged broad shoulders and said, "Then they discover it."

"And you will be forced to leave."

Ridge's eyes narrowed as understanding washed over him. She hadn't asked him if discovery would force him to leave; she stated it. Could it be that her fear was not of his father, of the possibility he owned a whiff of his father's bad character? Could it be she was simply afraid he would abandon her?

"No," he said. "I will not leave if I am discovered. If I am discovered, then I am discovered, and I will simply have to prove to those around me that I am an equal to them. I will simply have to find a way to keep my father's will at bay."

Ember felt her body begin to tremble, for her soul knew he was telling the truth. He would not leave merely for being discovered. It was not a promise that he would not leave for another reason, but he was assuring her that the discovery of his true identity would not strip him from her.

She was nearly moved to her own confession—to telling him of Selkirk and her shattered heart. She knew then he would understand her fears. Yet he would likewise know that she had silently admitted to loving him. She was still too fearful to confide in him—fearful that he might find disgust in knowing she'd loved another man, fearful that confessing to him would free her heart to fully loving him, revealing her as vulnerable to further pain—much greater—far more excruciating pain than she had ever known before.

Ember knew doubt must still linger in her eyes, though it was self-doubt, not doubt of Ridge's determination.

"Please, Ember," he pleaded, his eyes lingering on her mouth. "I beg you to believe in my sincerity. I am no villain."

She stroked his face once more, and this seemed to encourage him. In fact, he was enough encouraged that she saw the mischief return to his eyes.

"I'm no villain, Ember Taffee," he said. "I'm a merman...not a pirate," he teased, smiling. Ember giggled as he added, "Though I still maintain a pirate owns more masculinity than a merman." He shook his head, and she threw her arms around his neck. "But even still, I...I just can't see the compliment in being compared to a fish."

Oh, how he adored the sound of her laughter! How he reveled in the feel of her body pressed against his!

Ridge sighed, relieved. He'd nearly lost his hold on her because she feared he would abandon her—not because he was Arthur

Westminster's wayward son. He loved her all the more for the fact. He breathed a chuckle as the realization of his own thoughts struck him. He loved her. He did! Though it seemed impossible, he loved her. And now she knew his secrets—all of them—and she had not rejected him because of them. She was fearful—fearful he would abandon her, yes—but somehow the knowledge of her fear only spurred him to more confidence.

For a moment the memory of Tempest's implication—that Ember owned scars borne of pain—entered his mind, and he wondered if it were these scars that fed her fear. Was she frightened that he would leave and never return to her? Was it the fact her father had gone to sea and never returned that worried her? Well, Ridge was not a sailor. He would not adventure on long voyages to be gone for months at a time or to be taken by the cruel sea. He was a merchant trader. Certainly merchants and traders—any men of commerce—found the need to travel at times, but not for months and not in raging seas the way a sea captain did. Any business that required he leave her would take him for only a short time. He would always return. Didn't she believe this of him? He mused that it was the sea that had brought him to Ember. Was she indeed fearful that it would take him from her, as it had her father?

But these were musings that would remain for further pondering. Ridge had been patient—waited all the long day—thought of nothing but his warm Ember mermaid! He'd pushed aside desire, weathered emotional empathy for Tempest's heartbreaking endurance and for Ember's loss of a beloved father. He'd confessed his greatest secrets, triumphed in the fact she did not run screaming from him. And now his impatience to know her kiss—the sweet pleasures of her mouth—was spent.

"I'm going to kiss you now, my pretty mermaid," he whispered into her ear.

Ember quivered as his lips caressed her neck. "You sound as if you're warning me," she giggled.

"Oh, I am," he mumbled. He took her face in his hands, gazed into her eyes.

"Why?" she breathed.

"Because I'm hungry for you, Ember," he nearly growled. "Ravenous…and I fear I might play more the pirate than the merman in kissing you this time."

Ember smiled, her heart pounding like a hammer on an anvil in her bosom! Her mouth watered as she looked at him, her arms and legs rippling with goose bumps! Her stomach leapt with such exuberance and so constantly over and over that she thought she might indeed swoon from the breathlessness it caused.

She stole a quick glance to the Dirk and the Mermaid—to Mermaid Rock standing like a sentry nearby. She thought briefly of the Dirk of Fortune, the infamous pirate of legend—thought what a handsome pirate Ridge would have made.

"I…I like pirates," she whispered, shuddering as his lips brushed hers lightly.

"Aye…then pucker up, my little mermaid matie," he said, mimicking the accent of a sea-roughened pirate.

His mouth crushed to hers then, fairly sucking the very life's breath from her body to be replaced with an ambrosial atmosphere that tempted her to the very depths of submission and desire.

Ridge was ravenous indeed! As his powerful arms drew her against him—held her form firm against the sculpted contours of his body—as his mouth endeavored to quench some voracious thirst for her kiss, Ember surrendered to his will.

Heated, wet, avaricious—Ridge's kiss consumed her! There was nothing in all the world in that moment save him—Ridge, and her desire to be the conferee and bliss-bound beneficiary of his affection. There was no fear in her—no memory of Selkirk Beacon and the sting he had inflicted to her tender heart. No, there was only Ridge—his beauty of body and spirit, his kindness and wit.

"Slap me if I press you too unsuitably, Ember," he panted, having broken the seal of their lips for a moment.

"You wouldn't," she told him in certain confidence.

He breathed a chuckle. "Perhaps a merman wouldn't," he teased. "But a pirate might."

His mouth was at her throat, trailing soft, moist kisses along her sensitive flesh. The sea was calm. Gentle waves broke over the sand at their feet.

Breathless, Ember took his handsome face between her hands. She shuddered when she saw the smoldering fire of desire in the beguiling depths of his blue eyes—desire for her. She wondered whether he could read her passion through the windows of her own eyes as well as she could determine his. Yet her wonderings were answered a moment later, for Ridge's mouth found hers again, and Ember melted to him—melted to his will as surely as her mouth melted to the blending of their shared affection.

CHAPTER SEVEN
THE DIRK AND THE MERMAID

"I swear," he breathed, "I swear I'll ravage you if I don't put you away from myself this minute."

Ember heard a low, predatory growl rumble in Ridge's throat as his embrace slackened.

"Well, pirates do have a nasty reputation for ravaging women," Ember sighed, stepping back and out of Ridge's arms.

His chest rose and fell with the labored breathing of the forced dissipation of passion. He raked a strong hand through his ebony hair and chuckled. "And mermaids?" he asked, smiling at her. "Don't they have a nasty reputation as well? For leading men to their deaths with their powers of seduction?"

Ember giggled. "Oh, for pity's sake, Ridge West. I could no more seduce you than I could take flight with the gulls." It was not the truth, and she knew it. Still, she thought a feigning of ignorance might help ease their desire.

She watched as Ridge stooped, picked up a rock, and heaved it out to sea. She felt her eyebrows arch in admiration. The distance he'd thrown the rock was sure proof of the strength in him.

He exhaled a heavy sigh and glanced about. "This is a very secluded spot, this cove," he mumbled.

"Yes," Ember affirmed. "It's the cove of Mermaid Rock. I'm sure you remember it from before."

He frowned, looking rather puzzled. "From before?" he asked.

"Yes," Ember giggled. "You've been here at least once before…with me."

"I have?" he asked.

Ember was delighted! He was truly puzzled.

"The day…the day I caught Lily reading my diary about…about the day I found you."

An impish grin spread across his handsome face. "The first day I kissed you," he said. "Was that here?"

Ember nodded. "Yes—though the tide was in, so we were much further up, closer to the rock itself." She turned and pointed to the Dirk and the Mermaid.

Ridge chuckled. "Do you see how distracting you are to me, Ember Taffee?" he asked. He shook his head. "I swear I don't remember seeing that rock formation before."

"Well, it's not overly large—no larger than two people, of course," she said.

"Of course?" he asked.

"Yes," she giggled. "After all, it's not really a rock…not a natural one anyway."

"It's not?"

"No," she answered. "It's a man and a woman—a pirate and a mermaid, if you believe the legend. It's called the Dirk and the Mermaid, or Mermaid Rock."

Ridge's mind was beginning to win over his residual passion, and the name of the rock formation struck him like a thunderbolt. Mermaid Rock—the cove—the place where Tempest and her young sailor Seward had had their final rendezvous.

"Can you see them?" Ember asked him.

"See whom?" he asked in return, still distracted by the realization of what Tempest had confided in him.

Ember giggled. "The pirate and the mermaid, sir! There." She pointed to the rock, and his attention followed her graceful gesture. "Do you see them? Two bodies, a man's and a woman's. Their arms are entwined in passion's embrace. He's kissing her. Do you see their heads? Their arms?"

Ridge moved, stepped aside, and continued to study the rock formation. Slowly he did begin to see it—almost as if the rock were more a sculpture of a man and a women embracing instead of a random chance act of nature.

"Yes," he admitted. "I see them now—heads together, arms entwined, bodies pressed flush. The wind has her hair at her back."

Ember giggled, and the sound washed over him like warm honey. "Exactly!" she exclaimed. "Do you see that he has legs? But she—"

"A fin," he finished. He was astonished then. The rock formation above them on the shore looked exactly like a man and woman— rather a man and a mermaid—lovers entwined in passion's throes.

She clapped her hands with delight, giggling, and he could not help but chuckle, delighted by her amusement.

"Yes! Yes!" she applauded. "I knew you would see it!"

"So, it's a man and a mermaid," he mumbled. "Mermaid Rock. Yet you called it something else. So did your mother."

"The Dirk and the Mermaid," she confirmed.

"The Dirk?" he asked.

"Well, Mr. Pretty Treasure of the Sea," she began, "speaking of pirates, perhaps I should tell you the legend of Mermaid Rock—of the Dirk and the Mermaid."

Ridge could not resist the urge, the need to touch her. Reaching out, he caressed her cheek with the back of his hand.

"Oh, you should tell me," he said. "It would be wise for you to attempt to distract me…for our previous endeavors have quite got me thinking like a pirate where you are concerned."

Ember smiled at him. She adored his flirtations! Still, she knew there was wisdom in keeping his kiss at bay for a time. Taking his hand, she led him closer to the rock. "His name was Captain Dirk Bonnet," she began, "though he was commonly known simply as the Dirk— the Dirk of Fortune, to be exact."

"The Dirk of Fortune," Ridge mumbled. He looked at her and smiled with approval. "It's a good name for a pirate."

Ember smiled. "Yes, it is. And the Dirk was as infamous as pirates come. He lived a life of adventure, greed, sailing the seas in search of gold and jewels, ale and wom…"

Ember blushed as Ridge smiled and offered, "And women?"

She nodded. "Yes."

He nodded that she should continue, and she did. "It was said Dirk Bonnet was ruthless, wealthy, and wanton, that his heart was made of coral instead of flesh—brutal and spiny and unable to hold compassion or love." Ember sighed, for she loved the tale of the Dirk of Fortune and his mermaid. "However, it was also said that the Dirk of Fortune was as handsome as Adonis himself, owning such powers of seduction that even the most pristine of women could not resist or deny him." Ember felt herself blush again. "I should not be speaking of such things to you perhaps," she said.

"It's a story," Ridge said. "You've told it to others. It's well known in these parts. Why shouldn't you tell it to me?"

Ember shrugged. "I…I don't know. I just feel…somehow…"

"The Dirk of Fortune was handsome as Adonis himself, with such powers of seduction that even the most pristine of women could not resist or deny him. And then…" Ridge prodded.

Ember smiled and, though still blushing, looked to Ridge. The silent thought traveled through her mind that the handsome Adonis, Dirk Bonnet, could not have outshone either Ridge West or Chamridge Westminster. No, indeed not!

"Well, it is said the pirate was so handsome and strong that the three Fates themselves were drawn to the Dirk of Fortune," she continued. "He was too beautiful to be damned, or so the Fates established. They could not bear to see him spend all eternity in paying for his sinful ways. They determined to save him—further, to keep him for themselves."

"Hmm," Ridge mumbled. "To seduce the Fates themselves…the Dirk of Fortune must've been something to behold indeed."

Ember smiled and nodded. "So the legends say."

"So the Fates, they chose to intervene on behalf of the pirate?" he asked.

Ember nodded. "Yes. They called to Neptune and asked for his assistance. 'Give us of yours,' they begged. 'Give us your loveliest mermaid, one whose siren song will capture and hold one so strong and unfeeling as the Dirk of Fortune. Ensure she has the purest heart, that she might change the Dirk's heart to flesh, that he may cease in his wicked and willful ways and be saved from eternal agony in order that he may dwell with us.' That is what the Fates asked of Neptune."

"And he agreed?" Ridge asked.

"Yes...and no," Ember answered. "He agreed to send a mermaid to lure Dirk Bonnet. Yet Neptune is not king of the sea for the sake of weakness...no. Neptune is powerful, cunning, and ofttimes selfish. He demanded his own provisions. He would send a mermaid—the loveliest and kindest in all the sea, Cordelia, which literally means—"

"A jewel of the sea," Ridge finished. He grinned triumphantly, and Ember giggled.

"Yes," she said. "Cordelia. Neptune agreed to send Cordelia to lure Dirk Bonnet away from piracy and lasciviousness, but on one condition. If Dirk Bonnet fell in love with Cordelia, if she likewise fell in love with him—and it must be true love between them—if they fell in love, then Neptune would own the Dirk, and the Dirk of Fortune would spend eternity with Cordelia instead of belonging to the Fates."

"An interesting twist indeed," Ridge said.

"The Fates were desperate for Dirk to be saved. Thus, in their desperation, they agreed to Neptune's terms. After all, many were the sailor who loved a mermaid, even followed a mermaid to the bottom of the sea and owned death for it. Still, mermaids are more often than not fickle...of course."

"Of course," Ridge chuckled.

"The Fates did not concern themselves that the mermaid might fall in love with the Dirk, and so they agreed, struck their bargain with Neptune, and Neptune sent Cordelia to lure Dirk Bonnet from his damning ways."

"And did she?" Ridge asked. "Did the mermaid Cordelia lure the pirate?"

Ember nodded. "She did, for she was the most beautiful mermaid in all the water of the world, with eyes as green as seaweed and hair the color of the coral sunset. And her siren song was as beautiful as her form.

"Cordelia waited for a night when Dirk was on the deck of his ship, exactly at the prow, and that was when she began to sing. Dirk Bonnet saw Cordelia there in the waves, and he was smitten by her beauty. Cordelia spoke to Dirk, telling him that, at the full moon, she could come ashore and meet with him. If he would wait for her here, on this very spot, she would meet with him when next the moon was full. Dirk agreed, of course, for what man could resist the chance to woo a beautiful mermaid?" Ember smiled when she saw that Ridge was entirely enthralled in her story.

"And?" he prodded.

"And for all that month long—as the moon was only a sliver in the midnight sky, then a half—all that month long the pirate Dirk Bonnet and the beautiful mermaid Cordelia would meet each night, Dirk on the deck of his ship, Cordelia riding the waves of the sea. Each night they would meet and talk, converse of the stars and sea, exchanging tales of humans and merfolk. And all the while Dirk was falling in love with Cordelia…which was expected. Yet what was not expected was that likewise all the while Cordelia was falling in love with the Dirk. Neptune watched with delight, with anticipating triumph, while the Fates watched merely with hope that Dirk would abandon his wicked ways so that they might own him.

"But then the night of the full moon came, and here, on this very shore, Cordelia walked from the sea." Ember paused and looked from the sea to Ridge. "They have legs at the full moon, you know…mermaids."

Ridge nodded, grinning. "So I've heard."

"Cordelia walked from the sea to find Dirk Bonnet waiting here. He'd taken a skiff from his ship to the shore, and there they met...touched for the very first time," Ember explained. She sighed. "How desperate they must've been to finally touch...to feel the warmth of one another. Can you imagine it?"

Ridge nodded, and Ember smiled, continuing, "They were lovers at once. Of course, they had been before, yet now they could touch, know that one another truly existed, that their dark rendezvous had not been merely the stuff of dreams. And with that first touch..." Ember was lost in the story, so lost she reached up, letting the tips of her fingers trail along Ridge's jawline. "With that first touch, Dirk Bonnet's heart of coral was turned...softened to flesh," she whispered. "With that first touch," she continued, her fingers trailing over Ridge's throat, "Cordelia's own heart melded to Dirk's existence. A mermaid is a woman, after all, and a man can own a woman's heart...hold it fragile, vulnerable in the palm of his hand." Ember dropped her hand from Ridge, more for the sudden and unexpected memory of heartache than for actual recognition she'd been caressing him.

"They fell in love," Ridge mumbled.

Ember nodded. "They did, and they met here each full moon for over half the year. Each night Cordelia would swim among the waves. Dirk would call to her from the prow of his ship, and they would talk—talk of their love and of the next full moon, dreaming of the moment when they would be able to touch once more."

"And what of the Fates and Neptune?" Ridge asked. "If Dirk and Cordelia were truly in love, then Neptune had triumphed."

"Yes," Ember said, glancing back to the rock formation before them. "Neptune told the Fates he would expect the Dirk to enter the sea with Cordelia when he left his ship on the eighth full moon of their meeting. Dirk was planning to leave. His crew was close to mutiny, for they were pirates and could not bear to see their captain reforming, for reform he did because of Cordelia's love. Thus, Dirk had promised Cordelia that on the eighth full moon since their first meeting he would abandon his ship and crew, find honest toil until they could find a way to be together always. The Fates, though glad in Dirk's reformation, were furious at Cordelia's having fallen in love with him. They argued with Neptune—said they would not send the Dirk of Fortune to the sea, that they had only saved him for themselves, and that they would not give him up.

"Neptune, however, is oft prevailing, and when provoked to anger, such a rage overtakes him as to cause the most violent of storms to rise. He said he would have the Dirk and Cordelia. He would see them to the sea. Yet the Fates argued they would not give him up, that they would do whatever need be to keep him from Neptune's realm.

"Therefore, on the eighth full moon since Neptune had sent Cordelia to Dirk, the jealous Fates intervened once more. Neptune had demanded that if the Dirk and Cordelia fell into true, true love, they would spend eternity together. And so the Fates, cruel and selfish as they sometimes are known to be, waited. They waited for the Dirk and Cordelia to arrive on the shore. 'You have won,' they called to Neptune. 'The pirate and the mermaid, they are lovers, and we will honor our agreement with you. Dirk Bonnet and the mermaid Cordelia shall spend eternity together indeed! For we shall turn them to stone this very night…and stone they shall remain for all eternity!'

"Neptune was furious! He shouted back to the shore, to the Fates. 'Wicked Fates!' he roared. 'You dare to provoke my wrath? I cannot keep you from turning Dirk Bonnet and Cordelia to stone! But I will set my own will to it. They shall be free, turned to ocean flesh, when thrice they have witnessed a love as true as their own. Turn them to stone if you will! But they shall be freed to live in the sea when thrice true love has been presented!

"As they lingered together on the shore, the Dirk of Fortune and Cordelia saw the storm rising. The sea began to boil, and Cordelia knew Neptune's wrath was provoked. Though she did not know of the argument ensuing between the Fates and Neptune, she knew an ill will was approaching. 'You must go inland!' she told Dirk. 'Neptune is in a fury, and the waters will rise! I cannot venture past the sand when he is in such a temper!' But Dirk so desperately loved Cordelia that he pronounced, 'I shall never leave you again, my love! Let Neptune send up what he will. I will never leave you again! I will return to the sea with you, and perhaps he will turn me to a creature of the sea, for I do not care to live without your touch…not another day!' Instantly, they embraced, sharing the kisses born wholly of true love and flaming passion. And it was in that instant that the Fates caused the elements to bear stone, stone to encase the lovers…forever. As Neptune raged from his throne on the frothy seas, he tried to steal Cordelia back to the sea. Quickly he held out his triton, turned Cordelia back to a mermaid. Yet the stone was fast and strong, encasing the lovers before Neptune could pull Cordelia from her lover's arms…entombing them even as they drew their last breath with a shared kiss of true love.

"The Fates laughed. 'If we cannot have him, neither shall you, god of the sea!' they shouted to Neptune. 'Yet I shall have them both!' Neptune roared. 'When thrice true love has known them, the stone will crack and release them, and they shall dwell in the sea together for all eternity…and you will never behold Dirk Bonnet!'

"Neptune sank into the depths of the raging ocean then, and the Fates mourned the loss of their pirate love." Ember paused, looking to Ridge as he stood studying the rock. "And here they are. Here, before you," she said. "The mermaid and the pirate…forever embraced in passion's kiss."

Ridge said nothing, only continued to study the rock.

Ember studied it as well. It was true she'd spent hours in study of the extraordinary rock formation, for it did indeed look exactly like a man embracing a woman—a woman owning a fin instead of legs. It looked exactly like two lovers sharing an impassioned kiss. Even the size of it was correct. Ember fancied in that moment that were Ridge to reach out and gather her in his powerful arms, he might be the exact size of the stone edifice of the Dirk of Fortune and she the mirror of Cordelia. The contemplation caused goose bumps to prickle her arms and legs, and she glanced to the sand near the base of the rock, determined to look for treasure and distract herself from any impassioned action toward Ridge.

Ridge studied the structure. It was incredibly intriguing. Certainly the story Ember had related was haunting and caused his mind to linger on fancy. Yet further he thought of Ember's mother, of Lily's father. He sighed, at once melancholy, next pleased that he knew true love had presented itself at least once in the presence of Dirk and Cordelia—wondering if the stone really would break away to reveal a pirate and his mermaid if twice more true love was shared in one manner or another in the presence of the rock.

"So these are the stories Mariner Taffee told, are they?" he asked, smiling at Ember.

"Perhaps," she said coyly. "Perhaps one."

"Do you believe it?" Ridge asked.

Ember looked up to him and smiled, for he wore no mocking expression—rather an expression of sincere curiosity.

"No," Ember confessed, though the confession saddened her. "Not anymore. Though I did believe it as a child when my father first told it to me." She paused a moment, thoughtful. "Still…" she began. Yet she did not finish speaking her thoughts aloud for fear Ridge would find her musings ridiculous.

"Still, what?" he prodded, however.

Ember shrugged, shaking her head. "I find so many mermaid tears here, just at the base of the rock," she confessed. "Almost as if Cordelia herself wept them…or perhaps her sisters of the sea. When I was small, my father would walk with me to this very place. He would tell me that Cordelia's sisters often came to visit her on nights when the moon is full. He said he thought the mermaid tears he and I often found here were theirs—the tears of Cordelia's sisters, evidence of their heartbreak at missing her so."

Immediately, Ridge looked to the sand at his feet, picked up a handful of it, and let it sift through his fingers. "I want one," he said.

"A mermaid tear?" Ember giggled. She was delighted that her story had so entranced him.

"Yes! I want one for myself," he mumbled, his gaze still searching the sand and rocks.

"They're very rare, you realize," she told him. She looked at her wrist, marveling anew at the beauty of the sea glass woven in the bracelet Ridge had gifted her. "Especially the blue ones."

"I still want one," he said. "How often do you find them here?"

Ember shrugged once more and reached down to pick up a small shell her eye had been drawn to.

"It's hard to say," she said. "The day I found you, there were five, in a small space of sand. I don't think I've ever found so many at once before. It was as if mermaids had accompanied you on the tide…perhaps wept at having lost you to the shore, as the Fates no doubt wept at losing their pretty Dirk Bonnet."

Ember studied Ridge for a moment. Oh, he was so handsome! So charming!

If I were a mermaid, I would weep over you, she thought. She likewise fancied that were she a mermaid, she would certainly use her own siren's song to lure him into being her lover—her husband.

She gasped, suddenly startled at her own ponderings. She knew Ridge cared for her, found some allure in her. Still, to think of marrying him…

"What?" he asked, having heard her gasp. He looked to her a moment. "Did you find one?"

Ember shook her head, and Ridge returned to his hunt. Her heart was pounding, her breath quickened—and not for her want to be in his arms but for the images splashing about in her mind! Visions of lying in Ridge's arms, of bearing his children—images of happiness and sunshine and joy—ricocheted about in her brain like sparks spitting from a fire!

He was near the base of the rock, and she heard him exclaim with triumph, distracting her from her dreaming thoughts.

"Cordelia has left a tear for me," he chuckled. She watched him use his index finger to dig something out of a small niche in the base of the stone. "See here?" he asked, holding his hand toward her.

Ember breathed a giggle. A tiny bit of cobalt sea glass settled in the palm of his hand—a perfect mermaid tear!

"Ooo! It's beautiful!" Ember exclaimed, trying to focus her attention on his find and away from dreaming. She picked the jewel up, held it high so that the now setting sun could kiss it. The lovely piece of ocean gem was nearly perfectly tear-shaped and smaller than most of the mermaid tears Ember had found. "The blue are my favorite, and they're more rare. I do think Cordelia herself meant you to have this one. I swear, it looks exactly like…like…"

"Like a tear," he finished for her.

She dropped the glass into Ridge's hand, smiling as she watched him study it.

"I can see why they fascinate you," he mumbled. "To think…to try and imagine how it came to be in the sea, how long it has been there, traveling to reach this very spot."

Ember giggled with delight. "Exactly," she affirmed. "Now you see why I like to wander along the shore. I'm nothing more than a treasure hunter, in truth."

Using his thumb, Ridge flipped the piece of glass high into the air, watched it glint in the dimming sunlight. He caught it once more, depositing it into the front pocket of his trousers. He smiled at her then, causing Ember's breath to catch in her throat. His smile was his own siren's song—his smile, his face, his existence.

"It's a marvelous tale," he said. "I can see why it has managed to hold your imagination captive for so long."

Ember nodded. "I remember when…" she began. Yet her words—her thoughts—were lost as she glanced to the horizon behind the mermaid rock to see a man standing atop the hill beyond.

"What is it?" Ridge asked, obviously having noticed the sudden frown puckering her brow.

"Just…just a man…there, on the hill," Ember said.

Ridge turned to look in the direction. He recognized the man at once—the battered sea dog who often lingered in town.

"Poor old fellow," he mumbled, raising a hand in a gesture of greeting. "What adventure and pain that old sailor has seen. I can quite imagine it."

The stiff-legged old sailor nodded a returned greeting and then turned and limped away.

"I've never seen him before," Ember said. "But somehow…somehow my heart aches for his weathering."

"Mine too," Ridge mumbled. "He seems to keep to himself."

He took hold of her hand then, raised it to his lips, and kissed it. His thumb caressed her wrist—traveled over the bracelet he'd given her. "It was he who made the bracelet," he said.

"The one-legged man there?" she asked, nodding to the crest of the hill.

"The very same," Ridge said. "But tell me when he's gone."

"He is already gone," she said. "Why?"

Ember thrilled and giggled as Ridge drew her into his arms once more.

"Because I am a pirate and you a mermaid," he said. "And I'll have one last kiss before returning you to your mother for safekeeping."

"But I thought you were my own kind," she teased. "I thought it was a merman I found on the shore."

Ridge scowled playfully—growled.

"Hold still, my beauty," he demanded in the roughened accent of a pirate, "while I kiss your fins off!"

Ember giggled with delight, gasped, and melted into oblivion as Ridge's lips claimed her own.

❧

"What has happened?" Ember exclaimed, worry, anxiety, and fear rinsing over her.

Lily was weeping, as was her mother.

"I'm afraid supper might be…might be a bit delayed, Ridge darling," Tempest said, looking to Ridge.

"Mother!" Ember cried. "What has happened?" She felt Ridge take her hand. She looked to him, frightened. His expression was not that of alarm, however—rather of calm, tranquil satisfaction.

"Good night, my warm, bright Ember," he said, kissing her gently on the mouth. "All is well, and it is an evening meant for the hearts of women."

"What?" she squeaked, though the serenity about him did soothe her somewhat.

"I'll have supper at the inn tonight, Tempest," he told her mother. Turning back to Ember, he said, "And I'll be here tomorrow, when business is finished for the day," he said. "In the meantime, I believe the Taffee women are in need of some privacy."

He kissed her cheek and strode away, toward town.

Ember didn't want him to go! She wanted him with her, wanted him to hold her. She was confused—still blissful from the moments spent in his arms in Mermaid Cove yet entirely discombobulated by the weeping of her mother and sister.

"Oh, Ember!" Lily cried, taking Ember's hand. "It's…it's so wonderful! So very wonderful, my darling sister!"

"What is so wonderful?" Ember asked, her mind whirling in a confusion of thought and emotion.

"Please may I tell her now, Mother?" Lily asked Tempest. "Now? This very moment?"

"Of course, my pretty Lily," Tempest whispered. "Of course."

"What are you going to tell me?" Ember begged. "What has you both weeping with what appears to be joy? Though I know of nothing that could cause—"

"I am not the daughter of the merchant Nicholas Alexander, Ember!" Lily exclaimed. "No, I am most certainly not! And it's why I can paint and draw, why my hair is dark…and my disposition often too gloomy!"

"What?" Ember breathed. She shook her head, nearly overwhelmed with perplexity. "What do you mean?" She glanced to her mother—fancied her mother's countenance held humility, fear, and gladness all at once. "Lily? Have you gone mad?" Ember asked.

She glanced up to see Ridge. He'd paused some distance off, seemed to be watching them. He nodded to her with reassurance—drew his hand to his lips, tossing her a kiss.

"I have not gone mad!" Lily giggled. "I have gone delirious with joy and relief!"

Ember watched as Ridge turned and disappeared into the coral shadows of sunset's twilight.

"Oh, let your lover go, Ember!" Lily exclaimed with delight. "He is no doubt weary from the day of business. And anyway, he can make love to you when I've finished explaining." Lily took Ember's hands in her own. "Look at me, sister," she demanded.

Ember obeyed and was awestruck by the twinkling light in her emerald eyes. She'd never seen such excitement in Lily—never!

"My father was Seward Conner," Lily whispered, brushing a joyful tear from her cheek. "He was a young sailor and artist, and he was lost at sea…just like our father was!"

"What?" Ember asked.

"I am your sister, Ember," Lily said, "your sister because we share the same mother. But I am Seward Conner's daughter, not Nicholas Alexander's. See here? Look, I have even the look of him, don't you think?"

Ember blinked as Lily drew a photograph from her apron pocket and forced it into her hands.

"Mother gifted me this just here, just moments ago," Lily said. "I strongly favor him in appearance, don't I?"

Ember gazed at the photograph of a young sailor—a handsome, dark-haired youth that did indeed put her in mind of her own sister. She glanced from the photograph to her mother—to her mother, who stood seeming frightened, as if expecting the worst of heartaches was about to crush her.

"Seward Conner," Ember whispered. She smiled and looked to Lily, tears filling her eyes at the sight of her sister's happiness. From the time Ember had been told that Lily's physical father was different than her own, she'd pitied her sister, for she knew Lily was sorrowful for having never been loved by Nicholas Alexander. The joy in her sister's countenance now was undeniable, and it warmed every contour of her heart.

"You do favor him," Ember said, smiling. She glanced at the photograph again. "He was very handsome…as you are very beautiful."

"Oh, Ember!" Lily cried, flinging her arms around Ember's neck. "I am your sister! Your deliriously happy sister…born of love and not necessity!"

Ember wept then, tightening her own embrace. She had no notion of what had passed between her mother and Lily while she'd been rapt in the wonder of Ridge's arms and kiss. Still, whatever it was, it had been healing for Lily. And though the whispers of her soul told her it had not been the same sense of healing for her mother, she knew it had soothed the pain of some deep tear in Tempest Taffee's heart as well.

Through her tears, she gazed in the direction Ridge had gone, longing to share the moment with him. She thought then that if Lily's poor heart could be mended after a lifetime of aching, then perhaps hers could be as well. It was in that very instant that Ember Taffee realized her heart no longer winced at the thought of Selkirk Beacon. Not a pinch—no discomfort of any sort. It was in that instant she realized Ridge West had driven out the heartache Selkirk had planted—completely driven it from her. Oh, her heart was consumed, it was true, but consumed by love—love for a handsome merman (or pirate) that Neptune himself had delivered at her feet.

CHAPTER EIGHT
THE MERMAN IN THE BOTTLE

Every evening Ridge journeyed to the cottage for supper. Every evening he and Ember would meander along the shore, or in the fragrant grasses on the hill above it, discussing their thoughts, opinions, and histories. Every evening would end blissfully for Ember—with long moments, minutes, or even hours spent rapt in the passion Ridge's kiss and caresses induced.

With each passing day, she loved him more, and her love had grown to a marked sense of obsession—of desperation! She'd begun to understand that she could not exist without him—not wholly, not happily or hopefully. This realization—these feelings of desperate love—often frightened her. Though her heart no longer ached at thoughts of Selkirk Beacon, her mind did. Always there were whispers in the dark corners of her worries, reminders that Ridge was Chamridge Westminster, that time and time again he'd been forced to move on for the sake of someone having discovered his true identity. The dark whispers fed her fear of losing her lover, the possessor of her heart and all its desperate, passionate love.

Ember tried to ignore the dark whispers, and when she was in Ridge's company, she was nearly able to block them entirely. It was for this reason—the fact that his company soothed and comforted her secret fears—that she often made the walk to town to lunch with him at midday. For the nearly two weeks since Ridge had abandoned the cottage for his room in the inn, Ember had often journeyed to town or just outside it. They would plan their rendezvous the evening before, and if Ridge's business seemed to offer an allowance of free time in which to take lunch, Ember would carry a picnic basket full of good things to eat and meet him.

In truth, Ember wished they would never have to be parted—not for one moment of the day—or the night. Still, her rational thoughts confirmed life required lovers to be apart at times and that the time apart only sweetened their time together. Thus, Ember hoped Ridge would not leave her or be taken from her. Hence, she allowed herself to fall deeper and deeper in love with the handsome gift Neptune had left her on the shore.

Ember kissed Ridge. Breaking the seal of their lips, she took his face in her hands and studied him. "You're overly tired this evening," she told him. Gently she smoothed the weary furrow between his brows—frowned when she noted his eyes did not hold the same merry light they usually did. Dark circles beneath them also revealed great fatigue.

"I'm fine," he said, smiling at her. "It was just…just a very long day. Morgan had a new ship in port. It was early, and we were not expecting it. The cargo had to be unloaded, and we were shorthanded." He chuckled, and she recognized he was about to tease her. "Still, the more labor my body does, the more muscles I build, which makes me stronger…which makes you less able to avoid my advances." He bent, placing a moist, lingering, entirely affecting kiss to one side of her neck.

She giggled and delighted at another moist kiss at her throat.

Still, she was concerned for him. Taking his face between her hands once more, she forced him to cease in kissing her neck—to look at her. "You need your rest," she told him. "It frightens me to see you so worn."

"I'm fine, pretty mermaid," he said, tucking a strand of hair behind her ear. He grinned, revealing a heightening mischief. "But if you're so worried about me, why don't you bed me yourself? That way you could be certain I would sleep a little." He grinned and whispered, "Or not at all."

Ember gasped, feigning chagrin at his insinuation. She silently scolded herself for the warm thrill that traveled down her spine, however, as she scolded, "Ridge West! What a thing to say! Now I know you're overly tired. You get back to the inn and go to bed."

He chuckled. "I don't really have to get back to the inn to go to bed."

"Ridge!" Ember gasped. "You can't say things like that!"

"Why not?" he teased. "I think them."

"You can't say everything you think!"

"I don't," he said. His smile broadened, and he added, "Believe me…I don't."

"You're trying to seduce me," she said, wagging a scolding index finger at him.

He smiled. "Is it working?"

Ember giggled, took his hand, and began leading him back toward the cottage. "You're too tired," she said.

"So you *are* leading me back to the cottage," he chuckled. "Though I don't know if Tempest will allow me to—"

"Stop it!" she scolded, still thoroughly delighted, however. "*I'm* going to the cottage. *You're* going to your room at the inn."

"Maybe I should secure my own cottage," he mumbled. "Then I could drag you there and—"

"Maybe you should stop teasing me!"

"Who says I'm teasing?"

"Oh! You're completely incorrigible!" Ember exclaimed as she continued to lead him toward the cottage. He chuckled, and she noted how purely delighted her entire being was by the comforting sound.

Suddenly, Ember slowed her pace. There was a man standing on the hill above the shore before them. She recognized him as the same man she and Ridge had seen the day they'd been lingering near Mermaid Rock—the day she'd told Ridge the legend of the Dirk and the Mermaid.

Instantly her heart knew a measure of sympathy, for the man was ragged in appearance. His clothes were old and tattered, his hair long—black and gray like salt and pepper, as was his beard. He wore a length of crimson scarf tied about the top of his head, and it hung down his back, giving him quite the look of being an old scallywag or even a pirate. The dark of the evening and his thick facial hair masked the features of his face, but Ember could well imagine the weathered condition of it.

"It's the old sea dog from town," Ridge said.

Ember slowed her pace and dropped back a step to be closer to Ridge. "Is he safe?" Ember asked.

"What does your instinct tell you?" Ridge asked. "Though he does not put me in any state of worry. He never has. He seems a good fellow. He won't beg in town, not even for food, though I know he lingers in hardship. He'll only accept payment for the wares he barters with."

"And how do you know so much about him?" Ember asked, smiling. She adored that Ridge had taken such an interest in the old vagabond. His compassion—it was only one more reason for her heart to feel desperate in her love for him!

Ridge shrugged broad shoulders. "I've spoken with him, even shared a midday meal with him on occasion. He doesn't say much." Ridge raised Ember's hand to his lips and kissed the back of it as he traced the mermaid tear bracelet at her wrist. "But he's a fine craftsman."

Ember's hand burned with the sense of his touch—the warmth radiating up her arm and through her bosom. "And his name?" she asked.

"They call him Old Salt in town," he answered. "I've never pressed him for anything more. I just sit with him sometimes when the ships aren't in." Ridge chuckled. "And I've got enough trinkets crafted from the treasure of the sea to last *you* a lifetime."

Ember smiled. "And you call yourself a shrewd negotiator," she teased, her heart further warmed by the knowledge her lover was so tenderhearted.

"Hello," Ridge called as they drew nearer to the man. "Out for a breath of evening sea air, Old Salt?"

The mangled old sailor nodded—rather growled, "Aye."

Ember grimaced as the man leaned on a gnarled cane. He seemed uncomfortable, worn, and weary.

"I walked a bit further than I planned, merchant," the man mumbled.

"Then let me be your companion for the walk back," Ridge said. "I'm weary and could use some company to keep my mind aware."

"Aye, mate," the old sailor said. "A weary man walkin' a dark trail alone—it's unwise, and I'd be glad for your company, lad."

Ember looked to Ridge, and he smiled at her.

"Good night, my pretty mermaid," he whispered. He kissed her softly on the mouth and then strode to the old sailor. The weathered sea dog turned and started toward town.

"Thank you for the bracelet, sir. It's lovely," Ember called out.

The man paused but did not turn to look at her. "Aye," was all he said.

"Meet me for a midday meal tomorrow, Ember," Ridge called, stepping into a slow stride next to the limping old sailor. "I'm sure I'll have a ravenous appetite by then."

Ember gasped as she saw the old sea dog's shoulders bounce with a chuckle. Ridge glanced over his shoulder, smiling and winking at her.

"You've got to forewarn them...so they'll be prepared to slap you. Isn't that right, sailor?" she heard him tell the sea dog.

"Aye," the sailor chuckled. "Aye, that ya do, lad. That ya do."

Ember smiled as she watched Ridge thoughtfully slow his gait. She knew it was difficult for him to take such small strides. His legs were long, and she usually had to take two or three steps to match his one. Strolling next to a man who had such difficulty walking, and was probably tired himself, would find Ridge drawing on his own fatigued patience.

She wondered at the old sailor. She'd never seen him before— not in town, at least. She'd seen him on the hill above Mermaid Rock—thought she may have seen him once before, but she wasn't certain. Still, he didn't unsettle her, not any longer, not since Ridge had asked her what her instincts felt. She had not been able to look in his eyes, had little time to determine him, but she was awash with a sense of tranquility. Thus, she surmised he was harmless—just a weathered old sailor, too tired and maimed to sail the seas any longer.

"I've never seen Lily so happy," Tempest said as Ember entered the cottage. "I mean, just look at this painting, Ember."

Ember followed her mother's gaze and gesture. Lily's easel was placed in the middle of the kitchen, a freshly painted canvas perched on it.

"I've never seen her paint anything but portraits, not since she was a small child," Tempest said. "But look at this. Look at the colors, the pastels. I swear I feel like I could step into it, feel the sea spray on my face, the warm sunset on my skin."

Ember smiled and nodded. It was true! Lily had never painted landscapes or any visions of nature—only portraits. Yet here she had captured the sea, the shore, the pink sunset horizon in perfect hue and feeling. It was beautiful!

"It's an expression of her happiness, Mother," Ember said.

"I know," Tempest whispered. "But...but why did she only do portraits before? Why only faces and people?"

Ember shrugged. "Perhaps because that was what her heart clung to most—the people who loved her or that she thought brought beauty to her life."

"You're right," Lily said, entering unexpectedly. She stood for a moment, studying the painting. "I...I only wanted to cling to those who loved me. Nothing else seemed very beautiful to me—not the sea, not the flowers—only the faces of those who loved me...or the faces I found beautiful." She paused, smiling at Ember. "Like your merman. Ridge is beautiful. I knew he was. I knew he would make you happy, and that's what I saw in him—that beauty of his healing your heart." She giggled and added, "Though he is beautiful enough without any other reason."

"Yes, he is," Ember mumbled. Her insecurities were rearing, as they did every night when Ridge left to return to town.

Ember sighed. Glancing to her mother, she saw that Tempest seemed to be studying her, and it was well she recognized the expression on her face.

"Don't be afraid, Ember," her mother said. "You must be fearless in this love. We never know what life may bring—what mistakes and trials, what joy, what loss. But for all of it, it is life, and love is what makes us vulnerable and happy. It's what makes us human!"

Ember felt tears in her eyes as her mother gently took hold of her shoulders, peering into her eyes—into her soul.

"He won't hurt you, Ember," Tempest whispered. "Not willfully...or knowingly. Even if he's taken from you as your father was taken from me, it won't be his choice. You cannot miss what will be your greatest treasure in life simply because you're too afraid to give him your whole heart...your whole self."

"He loves you, Ember," Lily said, taking her sister's hand. Tears escaped Ember's eyes as she saw the tears in her sister's. "He started loving you the day you brought him here." Lily paused and then added, "And you loved him the moment Neptune set him on the sand." Ember gasped, sobbing as Lily embraced her. "Love him, Ember! Fearlessly! Desperately! Eternally! I know he loves you that way."

"He's never said it," Ember sobbed. "Not out loud. He's never spoken the words."

"He's waiting for your heart to accept him, Ember," Tempest said, her voice soothing and calm. "I know you haven't told him of Selkirk, but I also know he senses it...senses something has scarred your heart. Ridge is nothing if not concerned for you, if not hesitant to hurt you, even if the hurt is simply provoking a memory."

Lily released her, and Ember brushed the tears from her cheeks.

"Tell him about Selkirk, Ember," Tempest said. "Tell him the truth." Ember watched as her mother gazed lovingly to Lily. "The truth will free you, my darling. I know that now."

Lily smiled, brushing a tear from her cheek as she kissed her mother's cheek.

"I'll tell him," Ember whispered, though fear was raging through her like thunder. "I will tell him...tomorrow...though what if—"

"No," Tempest interrupted. "No what ifs. Ridge was meant for you, Ember, and you for him."

"I have a confession," Lily said then. "I...I was going to wait to gift you something as a present, perhaps on your birthday or for Christmas. But I...I think...I think now would be the best time to give it to you, if only for the reason that it may lighten this moment for us all."

Ember felt her brow pucker with curiosity as Lily hurried to another room. She returned with a painting, though it was masked by a large cloth, and her sketchbook.

"Look," she said, opening her sketchbook. Ember smiled as Lily's graceful fingers leafed through page after page of sketches of Ridge. The sketches began with a weary, sea-tossed Ridge West— obviously sketched the night Ember had brought him to the cottage. Sketches of his eyes, his whole face, his broad torso and muscular arms.

"I couldn't think why I was so obsessed with sketching him at first," Lily confessed. "I knew he was meant for you, and I was not envious of that. But he was so beautiful, so perfect, and I was driven to sketch him," she explained. She leafed through several more pages, all cluttered with images of Ridge.

"And then," Lily began, "that night after Mother told me of Seward Conner and her desperate love for him, I found myself lying awake long into the night, thinking on my father—of *our* father, Ember—of his love for us, for me. I was lying there thinking that he loved me as much as he loved you. I knew he did, even though he had not been the cause of my birth. I know he loved me, and I began to linger on memories of Father. I remembered how he used to play with me, bounce me on his knee, sing me to sleep at night. I remember the stories he used to tell me of the sea, of the colors of coral and shells, of the sky and water during a storm and during calm. I began to realize that, though Seward Conner may have given me the gift of being able to draw and paint, it was Father who taught me to see the beauty in the world and in faces. Our father, Mariner Taffee…it was he who taught me to see the lines of worry in a face I loved or the brightness of joy. He spoke to me of colors, described such brilliance of red and pink and green, and when he was lost, I only wanted to have him here—to hold his face in my hands, kiss his cheek, and know he loved me. It's why I only sketched or painted portraits. I couldn't see the beauty in the world…not with Father gone."

Lily paused and smiled. "Then…then I remembered one moment with him in particular," she continued. "It was the day before he sailed, the last day I saw him. We were in the cove, and he was telling me of the Dirk of Fortune and his mermaid. I was less than delighted, having heard the story so many times before, and I asked him…I asked, 'Daddy, why is it that Ember so loves the stories of the merfolk and the sea, of pirates? I like sea glass as much as anybody, but no one loves it the way Ember does. I like the stories too,' I said. Father laughed. I can still see the mirth in his eyes. He said he didn't know but that he thought you just owned a little more of his soul than I did. He said I was an artist in chalk, pencil, charcoal, and paints—that that was the gift God gave me, a joy I had been blessed with. He said God had chosen to give you the same gift He'd given Father—imagination and a pure love for the things of the sea. I remember he laughed then. 'Why, it would not surprise me in the least, my Lily,' he said, 'to find one day that your heart will be stolen by a poet and your sister Ember's heart to be owned by a son of Neptune—a merman or some sort of Adonis-like being!'"

Ember gasped, and her mother wept and laughed.

"It's how I knew Ridge was meant for you, Ember," Lily said. "Because our father prophesied it."

Lily went to the covered painting, drawing it fully into the kitchen. She smiled, and Ember thought she had never seen such a beautiful, truly happy smile on her sister's lovely face.

"You will think it silly, I know you will," Lily giggled. "But I know you will love it too…though I doubt your Ridge will like it."

Lily removed the seascape painting from the easel, gently set it aside, and replaced it with the covered painting. She removed the cover, and Ember gasped—giggled with pure and overwhelming delight.

"I give you, Ridge…son of Neptune," Lily exclaimed.

Tempest gasped as well, covering her mouth as laughter broke from her throat.

Ember was breathless, awed by the most beautiful portrait she had ever seen, whether painted by Lily or any other artist! There on the easel was the most beautiful painting of Ridge. His ethereal handsomeness was captured perfectly—his eyes the richest blue, like sapphires, as beautiful as they were in life. His hair was black as pitch, longer than it was in truth, wild as it floated upswept in the sea in which he lingered. Broad shouldered, sculpted muscles in his arms, chiseled torso and stomach—his stomach that melded flawlessly with the most masculine merman trunk and fins of gold and iridescent scales any imagination could muster.

"Oh, Lily!" Ember laughed. "He'll hate it! He'll absolutely hate it!"

"I know!" Lily giggled. "But what do *you* think?"

Ember covered her mouth, overcome by joy and delight, by the mythical beauty of the painting. She studied it—sighed over the perfection of Ridge's handsome countenance. The merman was painted seen beneath the water, in the depths of the sea, with coral on the sea floor, kelp and fish around him. In one hand, the handsome Adonis gripped a long golden trident. The scepter gave him the look of a powerful warrior king and caused Ember's heart to leap with wanton admiration. His other hand was upturned, emeralds and rubies and gold doubloons resting in his palm while other jewels and coins sifted from his fingers to float toward the seabed. But wait! Ember giggled as she realized the scene was painted within the vague shape of a glass bottle.

"I thought we could hang it above the hearth in your room," Lily giggled. "That way you really could keep him in a bottle on the mantel."

"Oh, Lily!" Ember breathed, tears brimming in her eyes. "It's perfect. It's beautiful! I've never seen anything that affected me the way this does."

"Save the merman himself?" Tempest suggested with a residual giggle of delight.

"Exactly!" Ember laughed as her tears of joy escaped her eyes to stream down her face. "Oh, Lily, thank you!" Ember cried, throwing her arms around her beloved sister.

"Tell him, Ember," Lily said. "Tell Ridge you love him! Tell him tomorrow, before another sun sets! Otherwise, he may murder me when he sees this."

Ember released her sister, gazing at the beautiful painting, nodding as her breath caught in her throat at the sight of its perfect beauty once more. "I'll tell him," Ember whispered. "I will." She turned to her mother. "I love him, you know…oh, so desperately, Mother!"

"I know, my darling," Tempest said, brushing the tears from Ember's cheeks with her gentle hands.

"Shall we put the bottle with your merman on the mantel then, Ember?" Lily asked playfully.

"Yes, at once!" Ember said. She giggled, adding, "Though I'll not manage a wink of sleep with such a delicious creature for company."

And it was true! As Ember gazed into the mesmerizing eyes of the son of Neptune in the painting before her, she thought it was good the creature had no voice—else she find herself entirely seduced to delirium.

CHAPTER NINE
TRUE LOVE PRESENTED

Ridge studied Ember. She seemed nervous—beautiful but nervous. He was certain something was pricking at her brain. He didn't worry that she'd changed her mind about him or that she was vexed or disappointed in any way, for he owned the pleasure of her mouth full half the hour before they'd unpacked her picnic basket and begun to nourish themselves with something other than passion.

He watched her now—the way her hands twisted the fabric of her skirt, the manner in which she kept biting her lower lip. The pink was not so bright in her cheeks as it usually was, and he did not miss the trepidation lingering in her dark eyes. He thought of the night her mother had told him her tale—thought of her mentioning that Ember too owned scars. Were the scars Ember bore deeper than he thought? He sensed she meant to tell him something, something he knew she'd been keeping from him. But this knowledge did not worry or disturb him. It caused hope to swell in his heart, for he knew his little mermaid had been holding her full heart from his reach, and he wondered if in revealing her scars she might be freed, the way her mother was freed by telling Lily the truth.

"You have something to tell me," he said. The words were out of his mouth before he could stop them.

"I...I think so," she stammered.

Apprehension gripped him suddenly. His heart—his very soul— knew that she loved him, yet a part of him experienced an instant doubt. What if he had been wrong in reading her countenance, her language, her kiss? No! She loved him! He was certain of it. It was true she hadn't said the words, but neither had he. Over and over—time and again—he'd longed to take her in his arms, press his lips to her ear, and tell her he loved her. But something had stopped him—the tremulous condition of her heart, as if a premature confession might break her somehow. And so he'd waited, had never spoken the words, though he'd wanted to, nearly from the moment he'd met her.

"Are you going to tell me that you don't love me?" he asked, half fearful of her answer.

"No!" she exclaimed, scattering his fear at once. "No! Of course not!"

He smiled, sighing a breath of relief. "Then nothing you could tell me—nothing you can say or even confess—should give you cause to own the sort of trepidation I'm sensing in you," he told her.

Again her hands began wringing the fabric of her skirt.

Ridge was stretched out on his side on the light blanket Ember had brought for their picnic. He propped himself on one elbow and studied her as she sat near quivering with anxiety.

"Mermaid," he said, placing a strong hand over her trembling, skirt-wringing ones. "Tell me what it is you want to tell me."

She looked to him, her eyes dark and void of sparkle. "That's just it," she whispered. "I don't want to tell you."

For a moment, a vision of Tempest and her young sailor—of their weakness—entered his mind. He felt anger, jealousy, and a deep rage beginning to rise in him. Yet he gritted his teeth—attempted to appear calm. If Ember's scars were caused by a similar failing, he would still want her more than he wanted his own life.

"The truth will free your mind, Ember," he told her—yet struggling to withstand whatever blow she was about to deliver.

"Will it free my heart?" she asked.

Ridge frowned. This was not the response he'd expected. "Tell me, Ember," he said. "Just tell me. What is it that keeps you from belonging to me…wholly belonging to me?"

"Selkirk Beacon," she said.

Ridge felt his temper, his wrath, igniting. It had been his worst fear! He felt his hand tighten over hers, even for all his efforts to remain calm. "He owns your heart?" he managed to growl.

"He once broke my heart," she said. "And he stole something else from me."

Ridge felt his teeth grinding. His jaw ached with restraining his jealousy and rage. "Your virtue?" he asked.

"No!" she gasped, shaking her head. "Oh no! No! You're the only man who could ever possibly seduce...who I would be ever be in danger of succumbing to when...I...I...no. No. Selkirk broke my heart...and he stole trust from me."

Ridge raised an eyebrow as his wrath began to recede, replaced by pleasure by her near confession that he tempted her. "Tell me," he said. "Tell me about this cad who left his brand so deep on your heart."

She seemed to settle somewhat, and Ridge was glad he had not lost his temper over his initial assumptions.

"I was sixteen," she began, "and Selkirk was twenty—a sailor but with a wealthy father, who only sent him to sea to teach him experience. His family lived here for a time, and we met."

"And you fell in love with him," he said. Though he did not like the fact Ember had cared for someone else—loved someone else— he was accepting. After all, in truth, he felt it was purely miraculous that she hadn't been married long ago, for she was the most playful, tenderhearted, and desirable of young women.

"Yes," she said.

She looked away—to the sea. He could see it was difficult for her to tell him of this Selkirk, not because she still loved the sailor but because she loved Ridge. Suddenly, he understood. Realization washed over him like a fiery epiphany. The sailor had broken her heart—crushed her. A deep and abiding fear of love resided in Ember now—fear of renewed injury, of heavier, more excruciating pain.

"Was he lost at sea?" he asked.

"No," she told him. "He just tricked me, that's all. I loved him, and he didn't love me. He pretended to. For a long time he pretended...told me that he loved me." She shrugged. "Maybe he did. He claimed to...even after..."

"After what?" he prodded.

"Selkirk's father sent him on a short voyage," she sighed. "He was gone only three weeks." She looked to him. "Three weeks. That's all it took for Selkirk to fall out of love with me...and into love with someone else. Three weeks."

Ridge's eyes narrowed. He knew Ember—knew the force of her emotions, of her heart and soul. Thus, he was certain Selkirk Beacon had nearly been the death of his pretty mermaid. He loathed the man for it. "And now you're afraid that I might go on a voyage...that my head might be turned by another woman." he stated.

"Or your heart," she confessed.

Ridge's heart was hammering so brutally within his chest he thought it might well erupt from his body! The time had come—the moment he'd been waiting for. He sat up and took her shoulders between his strong hands.

"I love you, Ember," he said. "I love you like no man on this earth has ever loved a woman! Give me your heart, and I will keep and protect it forever. I will never give it up! Give me your full heart, and I will shield it with my life. I will be your hero, your lover..." He paused, smiled. "I'll even be your damn merman if you like."

She smiled, and several large tears escaped her beautiful eyes as she pressed a palm to his cheek. "I love you like I've never loved anyone...not anyone," she whispered. "I love you, Ridge West." She smiled and breathed, "Or Chamridge Westminster. Whoever you are, I don't care. I just love you. You don't know how desperately I love you!"

"Yes...I do," he said.

He drew her face to his, consuming her mouth—savoring the moist, velvet warmth of her kiss. Ember Taffee loved him—she did! He could taste it in her kiss, feel it in the way her hands moved caressively over his shoulders, wantonly wove through his hair. He'd have to wed her soon—very soon! His desires to have her—to literally have her—were nearly too great to restrain any longer.

He broke the seal of their mouths, rising to his feet and pulling her with him. He was weak—he knew he was weak—and they were too secluded. He kissed her with ravenous desire, hungry for her returned kiss. He'd known that confessing his love would weaken him, but he hadn't known how weakening her confession would be. He trembled with craving, worried with each passing moment that he might not be able to put her away from himself.

"You have to go home," he breathed at last. "I've...I've got to get back."

Ember smiled, even for her disappointment at his ending their impassioned exchange. She pressed her face to the solid contours of his chest, smiled as she listened to the rapid beating of his strong heart. He kissed the top of her head, and for some reason a vision of Lily's painting entered her mind.

She giggled.

"What?" he asked. She marveled that he sounded near as breathless as she felt.

"I know you love me," she answered.

"How?" he asked. "Because I'm sending you home before I seize you here and now?"

"No," she said. "Because you're willing to be a merman if I asked you."

He smiled, chuckled, and softly kissed her forehead. "And with that...you've just preserved your virtue for one more day," he said. "Now go home, this instant, before I change my mind."

Ridge rather pushed Ember from his arms, but she was not offended. She could see the battle with restraint in him—could feel it in herself.

Quickly she gathered up the picnic blanket, folding it and laying it in the basket she'd brought. "You may love me, Ridge West," she giggled, "but we'll see if you still care at all for my sister once you've seen what she's painted for the space above my mantel."

"What?" he asked.

"You'll see…when you come to the cottage for supper tonight," she said.

She stood on the tips of her toes and kissed the slight cleft in his chin. He caught her quickly in his arms, however, pressed a warm kiss to her lips, and mumbled, "I love you."

"I love you," she whispered, breathlessly.

"Now, go," he grumbled. She smiled as he rubbed his temples for a moment. "In fact, why don't you run?"

"I'll see you as soon as your day's business is finished," she told him.

He nodded, shoving his hands in the front pockets of his trousers as if the gesture would keep him from reaching for her.

"Now run away from me, my pretty mermaid," he said.

Ember smiled—her heart pounding, her stomach fluttering, her entire body quivering. Ridge loved her. He'd said the words—spoken them at last! Ridge loved her. And she did feel free—free to love him, to fearlessly love him.

Ember inhaled a deep, cleansing breath of sea air. Ridge loved her, as desperately as she loved him, and she knew nothing could change it.

Ridge was not simply a little distracted when he returned to the docks. Rather he was wildly distracted! So distracted he'd almost made a massive negotiating mistake—almost traded some rare spice cargo for only half its value. Still, no matter how he tried, he could not push Ember from his mind. Oh, he never could push her from his mind—or his heart or desires—but most of the time he was able to settle himself enough to concentrate on business. This day, however, he struggled to function with any kind of orderly thought.

He surmised his thoughts were so thoroughly adhered to Ember because they'd verbally confessed their love to one another. It had been spoken aloud—the words had passed between them—and Ridge knew the fact would only cause his frustration and desire to increase. He wanted to see her every morning, the way he had when he'd been staying at the cottage. Well, not exactly the same way he had seen her while as a guest in her mother's home. Rather, he wanted to see her every morning, lying in his arms when he first opened his eyes. He wanted to linger with her every evening—talk and laugh with her—love her! He knew the verbal confessions of love had purely sealed them together somehow, bound them in a manner they had not been bound in before.

Still, Ridge was cautious, worried. Ember loved him, and he'd eased her fears. However, did she love him enough to determine he was the man she would want to...

"Lad? Boy?"

Ridge's thoughts were scattered as he realized someone was speaking to him. He turned, frowning slightly as he saw the old sailor, Old Salt, standing behind him.

"Me, sir?" he asked, still collecting himself—still trying to let go of his pondering where Ember was concerned and concentrate on the fact that something else in the world existed.

"Yes, lad," the old sea dog said. The man frowned, his dark eyes smoldering with agitation. "Your lass," he began, "is she safe at home this day?"

"My lass?" Ridge asked. "Do you mean Ember?"

"Aye...if she be the lass who wears the mermaid tear at her wrist, the one I made for ye," he answered.

Ridge felt his frown deepen. Something in his chest began to know a menacing sort of sensation. "She was here," Ridge said. "She brought a basket meal at midday."

Ridge's heart began to pound, for he did not like the expression of worry—of near panic on the old sea dog's weathered face.

"A ship docked late last night," Old Salt said in a lowered voice. "The Wayward Maiden. Do ya know it, lad?"

Instantly, Ridge felt the hair on the back of his neck prickle. It was well he knew the Wayward Maiden—the ship he'd jumped from in order to avoid capture, in order to avoid owing a debt to his father.

"Aye," he told the old sailor.

"Four men come ashore from the Wayward Maiden," Old Salt said, "four men that did not sail with her when she sailed at sunrise this mornin'. They're makin' no notice of themselves, but I am wary…for the sake of your lass." He paused a moment and then said, "The four sailors…they're here to overtake ya, but they heard tell of your lass, and it put me to thinkin' that they might—"

"Have you seen any of them the last half the hour?" Ridge growled. Ember! Ember had left him for the path toward Taffee Cottage not half the hour before! If they knew he loved her…

"No," Old Salt said.

"The constable?" Ridge asked.

"He's worthless," Old Salt growled. He patted the thigh of his stiff leg and added, "More worthless than I."

Ridge ran. He did not pause to glean further information from the old sailor. He simply ran—ran for the path leading to Taffee Cottage! His mind was on fire with fear, his heart pounding so brutal he feared it might drop him dead before he could reach the cottage and make certain Ember was safe.

Why hadn't he considered it? Why hadn't he considered that the crew of the Wayward Maiden might not be so easily convinced that he'd drowned in the sea? Why didn't he consider that the lure of capturing Arthur Westminster's son to hold for ransom might be worth sailing back up the coast in search of him? He hadn't thought of it because any common man—any man who wasn't used to swimming in the sea for a great distance—would have naturally been presumed drowned. The crew of the Wayward Maiden hadn't known Ridge was an exceptional swimmer. Thus, he'd assumed they'd assume he would never have made it to shore. He growled—let an angry roar burst from his lungs as he ran—disgusted at his own asinine assumptions.

A fear—a terror like he had never known—gripped him. What if the sailors had followed Ember? What if they'd captured her, planned to hold her for ransom—or worse? He felt tears welling in his eyes, fury racing through his veins.

"Ember!" he breathed. "Oh, God! Let me be wrong!" he prayed as he ran on.

❧

Her back was to the sea, but before her lay certain ruin or death! Ember tried to breath—tried to keep panic at bay. Yet how could she? The four men had made their intentions perfectly clear—their vile intentions! She'd felt them, sensed a menacing presence following her along the path toward home. At first, she'd been afraid to turn, to glance back, fearing that she might turn to find her sensitivity had indeed been correct—that there was a threat nearby. Still, she'd convinced herself for a moment that it was merely some wayward thought that had caused her to feel uncomfortable. Thus, she looked back—gasped with horror as she saw the four rough-looking men following her.

For long moments she tried to convince herself the four men were only traveling the same path as she, that they were simply making their way from one point to another. But her soul whispered, *Not so!* and she'd quickened her pace. She'd hoped that if she could make it to the cove, to the Dirk and the Mermaid, there she might find a place to hide, for it was well she knew the rocks—and hoped that the four men did not.

When she'd heard the men quicken their pace—begin to gain ground on her—she dropped the picnic basket she'd been carrying and ran. Ember ran as she'd never run before, her heart hammering with fear, her legs burning with exertion. Yet she'd managed to reach the cove before the men. They'd shouted at her, telling her to stop—that she could not escape them, that they knew who her lover was, and that the Westminster heir would no doubt pay handsomely for her release by doing whatever it was they demanded of him.

In the quick glimpse Ember had had of the four men, she'd instantly surmised they were sailors. Thin and tanned as leather, she wondered how they'd come by the knowledge of Ridge's true identity. Still, it didn't matter! Whoever the men were, they meant Ridge harm. Of this she was certain! They meant her harm as well, but it was Ridge's safety that most panicked her.

Still, as she stood with her back to the sea, the tide moving farther and farther inland, she began to understand the true severity of her circumstances. These men would take her. If she did not escape now, they would lay hands on her and hold her for ransom—or worse!

"You've nowhere to go, miss," one of the men said. "And you've no reason to be so afraid. It's Ridge West we want, not you."

"Speak for yourself," one of the men growled. The other two chuckled, and Ember knew she could not simply stand and wait for them to take hold of her.

Frantically, she glanced around her—to the sea at her back, the rocks and rock formations to either side of her. She'd run too far into the cove! If she'd stayed nearer to the Dirk and the Mermaid, she could've perhaps scrambled over the rocks to her right and hidden herself in the small cave on the other side. But now—now she was pressed to danger. If she entered the sea—tried to swim around the rocks—she might be injured on the sharp, jagged formations she knew were below the water's surface now that the tide had risen. Furthermore, the sea itself seemed restless. What if she could not swim well for the sake of her cumbersome clothing and the indifferent demeanor of the sea? For a moment, she wondered whether she could simply rush forward, slipping through their grasps to make it to the hill above the shore. Perhaps then she could run again, perhaps outrace them enough to cry for help when she was nearer to the cottage. Certainly only her mother and Lily would be at the cottage, but her father's pistols were there, and her mother owned a deadly aim.

"Come now, girl," one of the men coaxed. "Come along with us. We don't mean to harm you. We just want you to help us convince that rich man's son to barter with us."

One of the men lunged forward, taking hold of the front of Ember's shirtwaist. She gave a startled cry and pulled away from him. She stepped back, winced, and cried out as her foot slipped—slipped down the side of sharp rock. She stumbled and fell backward into the sea, the water to her waist.

"The sea doesn't scare me, miss," the man said, wading into the water. Ember felt tears spring from her eyes as she saw the fabric of the front of her shirtwaist in his hand—saw him toss it into the water as he reached out and took hold of her shoulders. Ember tried to step back from him, not caring if the sea swept her out of the cove. At least in the sea, she might have a chance. Still, her right foot would not obey. She tried to move it—winced at the pain of torn flesh. She was caught! Her foot was caught in a niche in the rocks just offshore! She couldn't move.

"He found himself a pretty one, that rich man's son," one of the men said, wading into the water to stand beside his collaborator. "I bet you taste as sweet as honey, now don't you?"

Ember shrieked—covered her mouth in astonishment as she saw the man gasp as he reached for her. His face went stiff, as did his body. He fell forward, facedown in the sea, a large knife protruding from his back.

"What?" the other sailor growled. He turned to look to the cove's shore, to the two other sailors waiting there.

"Ridge!" Ember cried. Ridge was there, in the cove! He was fighting with the two other men, pounding them with his fists. One villain fell to the sand, writhing in agony. Ridge put his foot on the man's head, forcing his face to remain in the sand—forcing the breath from him. Ember could see the man would be dead in another moment, smothered by the force of Ridge's anger and the sand keeping the air from his nostrils. But the other man slammed a fist to Ridge's lower back, and Ridge reeled for a moment—but only a moment. Even above the waves ushering the tide to shore, Ember heard the crack of the man's jaw as Ridge delivered a fracturing blow. The second sailor on the shore fell to the ground, crying out in anguish. This blow rendered the second man helpless, as the first, gasping for air, struggled to rise to his feet.

"I'll kill you!" Ridge growled. "Run…unless you want to die!"

Ember watched as the man still choking for breath assisted the other to his feet. He held up one hand to Ridge—an indication of forfeit. Ridge did not pause to watch their retreat. Rather he strode toward the water, angry—enraged.

The man still standing near Ember took hold of the floating body of his dead comrade. Pulling the knife from the dead man's back, he shoved the corpse forward. As the sea took the dead sailor, the one remaining villain stepped from the water.

"I'll kill you before I'll let you get away from me again, Chamridge Westminster," the man growled.

Ridge said nothing—simply stepped into the water, taking hold of the man's wrist. Before she could draw another breath, Ridge had twisted the man's hand, plunging the knife deep into the sailor's chest.

"Threaten me once," Ridge growled into the dying sailor's gasping face, "you live. Threaten me twice…you know pain." He took hold of the man's shirt, lifted him a ways out of the bloodstained water, and growled, "Threaten my lover…and you die."

With the strength and power of Neptune himself, Ridge heaved the body of the now dead villain into the sea. And the sea swallowed him, dragging him to its depths without mercy or pause.

The water was to her shoulders, but in that next moment, Ember cared not for her captive foot, for the fear still resonating through her. As Ridge reached out, gathering her into his arms and against the powerful protection of his strong body, she could only sob—weep with residual fear, relief, and love!

"They knew you!" she sobbed. "They meant to harm you!"

"Me?" he breathed against her hair. "Who am I when compared with you? Oh, Ember, I'm so sorry! This is…all of this is…"

But Ember would not listen to his claims of blame—no! She pressed her mouth to his, trembling as the moist warmth of his kiss served to soothe her almost instantly. Ridge was safe! He was well, alive, and no longer in danger. It was all she cared for in that moment!

"I feared…I feared I would not find you…that they'd taken you already," he breathed.

"No…no, you came for me!" she cried. "But how…how did you know to come?"

Ridge took her face between strong hands, gazing into her eyes. The moist tears brimming in the cool blue of his served to take her breath away, and she wept, for she could see how frightened he was—even yet.

"The old sea dog," he said. "Nobody takes notice of him, it would seem, yet he takes notice of everything. He told me about—"

A wave surged, raising the water to Ember's neck.

"Come on," Ridge said. "I'll tell you when—"

"My foot!" Ember cried, only then remembering she was imprisoned. "It's caught! I can't free it, no matter how I struggle."

"What?" Ridge asked. A frown furrowed his brow as another surge raised the water to her chin.

Panic returned! Ridge looked to the sea beyond Ember—to the rising tide. Less than five minutes would find her head submerged! Gulping a breath, he dived. The water was dark and wild, yet he could see her foot lodged in a tight recess of a rock formation. He took hold of her ankle—tugged mercilessly. He could not dislodge her foot!

His head broke the surface of the rising tide.

"I don't want to drown, Ridge!" she cried breathlessly. The tide surged, and he watched Ember close her eyes—hold her breath until the wave had receded and she could gasp.

He'd cut her foot off before he'd let her drown. He would! He wouldn't lose her! He remembered then, however, that his knife was in the chest of a dead man—a dead man long since taken to the sea. Even if he had been able to amputate her foot somehow, he had no means!

"You won't drown," he said. He gulped another deep breath and dove again. The sea fought him, desperate to claim the shore, as he struggled to free Ember's foot. Ridge could feel panic threatening to overtake him, but he continued to twist her ankle—tug at her small foot in trying to free it.

When he surfaced, it was to find Ember spitting water from her mouth as the sea overwhelmed her. She was submerged! She could no longer draw breath!

Ridge inhaled a slow deep breath and took hold of her head, pressing his mouth to hers, blowing air into her lungs. He didn't know how long she could hold the breath, but he prayed it would give him time—time to try and free her again. He'd draw breath for her until he died trying to save her!

He gasped and dove. Quickly, he unlaced her boot. Then, taking hold of her ankle with his full strength, he pulled—pulled with every muscle in his body, with every prayer of his soul! Ember began to struggle. No doubt the breath he'd breathed into her was spent. With one final effort, he felt her foot move—felt the rock begin to release her!

Ridge pushed himself to the surface, gasped a moment, drew a deep breath, and took Ember's face between his hands. She exhaled what little breath was left her, and he pressed his mouth to hers, filling her lungs.

He gasped above the water, dived, grasped her ankle with both powerful hands. He felt it then—another slight slip. He braced one foot against the rock claiming her and pulled. She was free!

Putting his hands at her waist, he lifted her body with every ounce of strength left in him. His head broke the surface of the water, and he wept in hearing her cough—her gasp for breath.

Still frantic, trembling, and weak, Ridge carried her further into the cove, collapsing to the soft sand at the base of the Dirk and his mermaid. He gasped for breath as he took her chin in hand. She coughed once but drew a deep and clean breath. He let his head fall to her chest a moment as he struggled to catch his own breath. It was only then he realized her blouse was torn, the front of it gaping open to reveal her corset beneath. He'd nearly lost her. Whether to blackguards or the sea, he'd nearly lost her!

Panting, he raised himself to study her face—winced when he saw her smile at him as she pressed a palm to his cheek.

Quickly he took stock of her, somehow afraid a piece of her might be lost or too damaged. Her bosom rose and fell with labored but healthy breathing. Both her arms were intact, and her stomach, hips, and thighs. A brutal scrape caused blood to ooze from her knee, but her legs were otherwise complete. He sat back on his haunches, taking her ankle in hand. Already it was bruising from being caught—or his efforts to free her foot. Still, it was not broken, and both her feet were where they should be.

A strange desperation mingled with overwhelming relief washed over him. Taking the bruised ankle in hand, he bent her leg—pressing his lips to her knee that was not bleeding.

A sudden sense of time being too short—of life being only a fleeting breath—caused the wild desperation in Ridge to soar. Lurching forward to hover over her on hands and knees, he shuddered as he took her mouth with his own! He kissed her hard, demanding a response, relishing the warm flavor of her mouth. She moaned, her weak arms encircling his neck as his free hand gripped her waist.

"Ember!" he breathed against her mouth, still overcome with fear and anxiety. He kissed the cool flesh of her neck—buried his face against her throat. Only heavenly intervention had saved her. Only deity could have guided him to finding her—to besting four able men—to freeing her foot.

"Oh, God!" he whispered, tears brimming in his eyes. "Thank you for her life!"

Ridge placed his hand on Ember's midriff, elated in the feel of it rising and falling with her breathing. She was safe—and he would have her! Nothing would take her from him! Nothing would keep her from him one moment longer.

Ravenous, he kissed her, desperate to taste her, own her, before some other disaster endeavored to strip her from him. He'd never wanted anything so desperately as he wanted the soft, beautiful creature in his arms! He thought his body might fly apart if he did not have her fully. He sensed the same wild desperation in her—the same desire and impassioned abandon. Her arms were around him, pulling him to her as they lay on the sand. She accepted his lover's kiss, the demands his mouth made of hers. Indeed, he found she not only met his kiss, but her own desires fanned the roar of the shared affection.

He could not draw an easy breath. His hands only wanting to wander from their place at her back and waist, he broke the seal of their mouths, panting with the effort of reining in his passion. He would not spoil her! No! He would not! He loved her too much, too perfectly, too wholly to risk her innocence further. He pushed himself from her, rolled to his back, and clenched his teeth as he fought to keep from her.

At once, a vision of Tempest and her young lover Seward Conner—Lily's father—filled his fevered mind. In those moments, he knew it was an even greater love that would keep him from Ember—a greater love than Tempest and Seward had shared so long ago in a moment of reckless abandon. He loved Ember—more than he loved his own life—and he would not betray her purity and trust. He would love her more than Seward had loved Tempest, no matter the mad desire burning in his mind and body.

Ember gasped for breath, for she did not want to give up Ridge's kiss, his caress, and his obvious desire. Still, she knew it was the strength in them both that had caused him to separate from her. She was well aware of what was in his mind, for the same was in her mind as well. She silently assured herself that she would never have given herself to him there—assured herself he would never have pressed to take her in that moment. Yet for all that her flesh should be cold from near drowning, it was not, for it burned from his touch—flamed with desire for him—and she knew they must not linger.

"You need to be dried and warmed. I have to get you to the cottage," Ridge panted. "Before I…before I…before I take to warming you myself." He stood, effortlessly scooping her into the cradle of his arms.

Ember collapsed against him, her arms clinging to his shoulders as he carried her, her face pressed to his warm neck.

She gasped when she heard a loud crack, as if something had struck or broken upon of the rocks. She looked back, half expecting to see some large piece of driftwood or debris from an ancient shipwreck had washed to shore. But there was nothing—not even the bodies of the two dead sailors Ridge had saved her from. No, Neptune had taken them—taken them to the bottom of the sea.

CHAPTER TEN
THRICE PRESENTED

"Tempest," Ridge began as Lily helped Ember out of her wet clothes, "will you give her to me? If Ember will have me...may I marry her?"

"Ridge," Tempest said, placing a motherly hand to his cool cheek, "calm yourself. Ember is fine. Because of you, she's fine."

"Because of me she was nearly—"

"Because of you, she's safe," Tempest interrupted. "Sit here, in front of the fire. You're so cold as to be in danger yourself."

Ridge did as Tempest told him—stood shivering before the warm fire burning orange in the cottage hearth. Still, he was undaunted. "I must have her!" Ridge growled, taking Tempest by the shoulders. "Don't you see? Life...mortality...it is so fragile, too fleeting to be wasted! I love her. You know I love her! I must have her. Nothing else matters—not the trial of wealth, nothing! I love Ember, Tempest! Give her to me as soon as she is well and able...and oh, please, God, she must be well and able. And when she is, I will marry her." He paused, his brow puckering into a frown. "I will own her if she will have me, Tempest. I'll have Ember for my own." He paused, straightening his shoulders with determination. "I'll have her...with or without your blessing."

He was somewhat calmed when Tempest smiled warmly up at him. "Of course you may have her, my darling," she said, "for you are her desperation in love. I have seen it in her eyes. She's never loved anyone the way she's loved you."

145

Ridge felt the pinch of pain in his heart, his fatigue, worry, and weakness causing a faint fear to whisper to him. He frowned as he mumbled, "She loved Selkirk."

Again Tempest smiled. "Yes, she did," she affirmed, causing the pain in Ridge's heart to grow. "Truly loved him...but not near so desperately, so perfectly as she loves you. You have driven him from her heart. Oh, he may always own a shard of it, for none of us ever truly ceases loving someone we once did. And it is because she loved Selkirk Beacon that Ember knows how infinitely more...how perfectly desperate she loves you."

"Forgive me, Tempest," he mumbled, even as he hoped. "But you cannot assume to know her mind...or her heart." Ridge knew Ember loved him. He knew it. But would she have him? Would she marry him? The events of the day had worn his body and mind, straining his confidence.

Tempest giggled, moved forward, and embraced him. "Oh, darling, I don't assume to know her mind and heart. I well know it, for she told me herself she is so desperately in love with you as to think herself overcome with insanity at times!"

Ridge sighed as Tempest released him, chafing his arms.

"Closer to the fire, darling," she instructed. "You're still far too cold for my mind to know any sort of ease."

Ridge did as instructed. He was cold, and the ill-fitting clothes he wore did little to change the fact. Still, he was grateful Tempest had kept her husband's clothes, for he was glad to have a dry set, no matter how ill-fitted they were.

He sighed, glancing to the back of the cottage with concern. "She's all right then?" he asked.

Tempest nodded. "She's fine," she assured him. "Lily will have her dried and dressed any moment. Then you can go to her."

He nodded, entirely impatient, almost frantic to see Ember again—to know she was indeed well. Ridge put one fist to his mouth, blowing warm breath into it in an effort to hurry the warming of his body. He glanced up then, to the portrait of Ember's father hanging above the mantel.

"Do you think your Mariner would approve of me, Tempest?" Ridge asked, studying the painting of the lost Captain Mariner Taffee.

"Oh yes!" Tempest said, following his gaze. "Mariner would have adored you! I can well imagine the camaraderie the two of you would have shared."

He frowned and asked, "Is this the same portrait that was here before?"

"No," Tempest answered. "This portrait used to hang above the mantel in Ember and Lily's room. Lily painted a new portrait for Ember, so we moved this larger one of Mariner here, and the one that used to hang just here is now with me in my room. Why do you ask?"

Something about the painting struck him—something he had never noticed before. "Your husband," he began, "he...he was missing a finger?" Ridge moved closer to the painting of Ember's father. The sailor in the painting indeed was missing most of one finger—most of his left ring finger. Ridge's eyes narrowed as he studied the finger more closely—as he studied the very familiar-looking tattoo at the nub of it.

"Yes," Tempest affirmed. She giggled slightly as she said, "He used to tell the girls he'd lost the finger in a fight with a pirate, though the truth of it is he caught it in a rope while casting off as a boy." She shook her head, sighing as she too studied the painting. She reached up and lightly caressed the place where the tattooed ring was. "After we were married, we found his wedding ring would never stay on his finger—rather on what was left of it. Always slipping off, it was. So within a month of our vows, he had this done...a tattooed ring. He said he wanted me to know he would've worn a ring for me if he could have."

Ridge nodded, gazing into the dark brown, the near black, of the sailor's eyes—Ember's eyes. This was Ember's father! This was the father who had so unconditionally loved Lily as his own. This was Tempest's husband and true love, and this—this was the old vagabond sea dog who lingered near town—who crafted sea glass into jewelry!

Ridge scowled, angry with himself for not having seen what had been put in his path for so long. The old sailor in town—Old Salt—was in fact Mariner Taffee himself! Ridge shook his head in awed astonishment, for there was even more that came into his mind now concerning the old man. Old Salt's wares—the ornaments and jewelry he sold—all made of sea glass! Bracelets, necklaces, and other trinkets adorned with mermaid tears—Ember's favorite treasure of the sea. It had been Ember's own father who had sold him the mermaid tear bracelet she now wore, Ember's father who had warned Ridge about the four sailors who had nearly taken her. The stiff-legged old sailor—the battered, weathered, worn man who often went hungry—Mariner Taffee! He saw it plainly in the painting—Ember's eyes, the tattoo on the finger nub, and his concern over the Taffee women. Ridge could think of several times that the old sea dog had been lingering above the shore near Taffee Cottage. Had he been watching over them? If so, how long?

Ridge remembered then—the merchant Morgan. Upon seeing Old Salt lunching with Ridge one afternoon, Morgan had asked if Ridge knew Old Salt before, for the old sailor had appeared only a week before Ridge had. Morgan was worried about the vagabond, that men traveling to the docks and warehouses might find him distasteful.

"Have you ever seen the old sailor in town?" Ridge asked Tempest.

She shrugged and shook her head. "No," she answered. "I so rarely go into town, though I've heard talk of him. It seems he peddles the loveliest ornaments made from the treasures of the sea. Mrs. Morgan was wearing the prettiest bracelet last week when I saw her, crafted of the loveliest pink shells. Why do you ask?"

"He was the one who warned me about the sailors from the Wayward Maiden," Ridge said. "He saw the ship dock, saw the four scoundrels stay behind when she sailed at sunrise. I...I have to thank him."

"Oh yes!" Tempest exclaimed. "Please thank him for me too, Ridge. Without him…I can't let my mind wander to what might have happened. Thank him for me. Ask him to supper!"

"I will," Ridge mumbled. He looked to Tempest—saw the gratitude, the desperate gratitude, in her eyes. He wanted to tell her—wanted to take her by the arm, drag her to town, and show her that her husband was alive! Yet he knew Mariner Taffee must have a reason for keeping himself from her, though Ridge could think of no valid reason himself.

"I've put her in a warm tub," Lily said, entering the room then.

"May I see her?" Ridge asked. His heart was pounding with anxiety. He had to know Ember was well! He had to see her—to hold her!

Lily smiled at Ridge and placed a tender hand to his arm. "As soon as she is warmed and dressed," she told him.

"I want her now," Ridge growled.

"I know," Lily said. "But she needs the warm bath. It won't be long. I promise."

Ridge was angry. He wanted Ember—wanted to hold her, to assure himself of her well-being. Still, she was not his wife yet. He knew he would have to wait until she'd bathed to warmth and dressed.

"I'm going to town," he announced. "I mean to thank the old sailor, to explain to Morgan…and to keep myself from bursting into that other room," he added, pointing toward the back of the cottage.

"I think that's wise, darling," Tempest said. "Ember will be fine, and when you return…"

But Ridge didn't wait for Tempest to finish. He stormed out of the cottage—enraged with Mariner Taffee, still frightened over Ember's fragile state.

❧

The run to town warmed him, settling both his temper and his fears. He paused only long enough to go to his room at the inn and dress in his own clothes. Then he went to the merchant, explaining what had happened with the sailors and Ember. Morgan was understanding, though somewhat aghast that such a thing as four sailors attempting to accost a young woman could take place in his realm of life.

"Miss," Ridge asked, bursting through the doors of the Sailor's Knot and addressing the barmaid there.

"Yes, sir?" the tart asked. She smiled at him alluringly, but Ridge's scowl only deepened.

"The old sailor...Old Salt," he began, "do you know where he is?"

The barmaid exhaled a sigh of disappointment. "I ain't seen him all day," she said. "But he stays in the shanty behind the inn. The innkeeper lets him sleep there."

"Thank you," Ridge said.

Ridge's anger began to grow as he made his way back to the inn. There was, indeed, a small shack behind it. Ridge had never taken notice of it before, but then again it seemed he hadn't taken notice of a lot of things of late.

He inhaled a deep breath, raised a fist, and rapped on the shack's crudely constructed door.

"Aye?" came a voice from beyond.

"It's Ridge West," Ridge rather growled.

He heard movement within the hovel, and then Old Salt opened the door. "Is she safe?" the old sailor asked.

"Ember? Yes," Ridge told him, "though you were right to own concern. They were fast upon her. I only just made it to her before they—"

"Did ya kill them, lad?" the old sailor growled. Ridge could see the fury in his dark eyes—his eyes that so resembled his daughter's.

"Two of them," Ridge confessed. "I only beat the other two."

Ridge was angry—angry at Mariner Taffee for not coming forward, for hiding, for not explaining to his family where he had been for fourteen years. It was obvious the man had been somewhere, and from his appearance, it had most likely been a miserable place. Still, Ridge did not understand why he had not come forward—yet simultaneously understanding that it was not his place to pass judgment on Ember's father.

"I've come to ask you for your daughter's hand, Mariner Taffee," he said.

Mariner Taffee's eyes narrowed. "Ya love Ember then?" he asked. His gaze did not leave Ridge's. This was a strong man, and Ridge was again struck with wondering at what had kept him from his family. Briefly he mused that perhaps Mariner Taffee had been like Selkirk Beacon—that another woman had turned his head. But Tempest would not love a man capable of betrayal.

"Do ya love her, lad?" Mariner growled, pulling Ridge's thoughts back to the moment at hand.

"You know that I do," Ridge said. He was careful to remain calm, though his temper was sorely pricked.

"And she loves you?"

"She says that she does," Ridge mumbled.

"Does she love ya, lad?" the man asked, taking hold of the front of Ridge's shirt. His dark Ember-eyes smoldered with pain and loss—fear.

"She does," Ridge answered. He drew a breath of courage and added, "I think she loves me as much as her mother loves you."

Moisture welled in Mariner's eyes. He sniffed and let go of Ridge's shirt. "Do ya think Ember would love ya if you'd been lost for near fifteen year?" he asked.

"I think she would," Ridge answered as understanding began to wash over him.

"And if you'd been pirated, set adrift, and imprisoned at Barbados fourteen years ago…if you'd spent more than a decade in a dungeon in a foreign land…if ya'd spent near two years in tryin' to return to her…do ya think she'd still love ya then, lad?"

"She is full her mother's daughter…Captain. She would love me after such separation and misery, just as her mother yet loves you," Ridge said. He was humbled beyond measure—scolded himself for the angry thoughts he'd owned of Mariner only a moment before.

The man's dark eyes narrowed once more. "You near took her to yarself just today…there, on the sand beneath the Dirk and his Neptune's maiden," he said.

Ridge felt the heat of discomfiture rise to his cheeks. It was true! Only his love for Ember had kept him from making her wholly his. He knew enough of this man through his wife and daughters to know Mariner Taffee would not have lingered in town, letting Ridge face the scallywags alone. No doubt he'd hurried after Ridge—after telling him of the danger Ember might have been in. No doubt he raced toward the cottage as fast as his stiff leg would allow. Ridge wondered how much of the struggle with the sailors Mariner had witnessed—wondered whether he'd seen Ridge's efforts to free Ember's foot from the rocks beneath the tide. Still, it was obvious he'd seen Ridge carry her to the safety of the sand—seen their passion erupting in full view of the Dirk and the Mermaid.

"Didn't ya, lad?" Mariner asked.

"Yes…but I didn't," Ridge said.

"And why was that?" Ember's father prodded.

"Because I love her—more than my own desire…more than my own life," Ridge answered honestly.

The man nodded, a smile of approval spreading over his weathered face. "That place, the stone, the Dirk of Fortune and his mermaid…it's not as private as so many people think," Mariner Taffee chuckled.

Ridge smiled as Ember's father winked at him with understanding. "So it would seem," he chuckled.

"And so Tempest and I discovered ourselves one moonlit evening long ago," Mariner added. He chuckled and offered a rather gnarled hand to Ridge. Ridge accepted his hand, surprised by the strength yet in it. "Marry her then, lad," Ember's father said. "And once she's yours, never leave her for longer than a day's work. The sea is not for lovers, lad. And it is cruel to the women who love sailors."

"I'm no sailor, sir," Ridge assured him.

Mariner nodded. His eyes narrowed, seeming to bore a hole straight through Ridge's soul. "Does Ember know who ya are?" he asked unexpectedly. "And, lad, do ya know that your father has passed away?"

Ridge went cold. His very flesh seemed to turn to ice over the muscles that bound his being. "My father?" he breathed.

Mariner Taffee nodded. "Yes, lad. I heard the yarn only moments ago. Arthur Westminster, the owner of the greatest shipyard to the south, has died. They'll have it in the papers tomorrow, no doubt." He paused, and Ridge could not speak.

Ridge could not take it in. Arthur Westminster was too severe, too cruel, and too powerful to be conquered by death. In truth, a part of Ridge knew a sad sense of respite of the soul. He would mourn his father in a manner, for the man had assisted in giving him life. Furthermore, he pitied him—pitied his rich, arrogant, stonehearted sire—pitied him for never having loved or been loved. He paused in thinking of his father—gazed at the weathered, worn man before him. Here was a man who had loved and been loved, who yet loved and was yet loved. Far better to die with the love owned by the man before him than the lack of it as his father had.

The world rarely missed such a man as Arthur Westminster. Yet Ridge knew two who would miss him—little Daisy and young Artie. Ridge had always pitied them in never knowing a mother's love, in never truly knowing a father's. He could not leave them to be raised by nannies and servants. It was not the life he wished for, not the life he would wish for them.

"Your choice to live a quiet life here in Ember's lovin' embrace...it is the best choice, the right choice, lad," Mariner told him. "You'll not regret choosin' love and honest labor over luxury and wealth. But then what of the two young ones your father left behind?"

Ridge fancied the man had read his mind—wondered how he knew so much about it all. "You seem to know a great deal about a man who has struggled long to keep his identity a secret," he said.

Marnier smiled. "Do ya think I'd be allowin' my daughter to fall in love with a man when I knew naught about him?"

Ridge's eyes narrowed. "Perhaps you're like your wife," he offered. "Perhaps you own Tempest's gift for determining a soul."

"Perhaps," Mariner said, shrugging broad shoulders. "Or perhaps I eavesdrop on solicitors meeting with castaways in the Sailor's Knot. Perhaps I'm wary of sailors—sailors from ships who tell tales of a rich young man of privilege working for passage down the coast. Perhaps I heard how the lad was found out by the crew of the Wayward Maiden, that it was discovered his name was Chamridge Westminster, that members of the crew threatened to hold him for ransom…planned to collect a fortune from Arthur Westminster, the great shipbuilder. Perhaps they spoke of the lad's strength, courage, and cunning, of how he jumped ship near Trident Point, how most of the crew knew the man could not possibly swim through such rough waters. Yet there were four who thought he might be just a man to make the swim…and survive. As for me knowledge of your wee siblings…well, everybody who knows of Arthur Westminster, knows there are two other heirs if the eldest heir does not come forward."

Ridge smiled and shook his head, entirely awed by Mariner Taffee's cunning. Yet in the next moment he thought of his own father. Arthur Westminster's death meant Ridge would be free! Yet as heavy guilt at the sense of liberation he was feeling pressed against his heart, a sudden and thoroughgoing concern for Daisy and Artie tortured him as well.

Ridge had long ago forsaken any want or desire for his father's unimaginable fortune. Yet his little brother Arthur, his gentle and pretty sister Daisy, they were but six years of age—unable to walk away from the corruptive life their father intended to drown them in. No doubt they would be managed by trusts, raised by servants— people who were being paid to care for them. Arthur and Daisy would know luxury and spoiling beyond imagine. There would be no tenderness, no teaching, no nurturing of the naturally kind, compassionate, and tender hearts of children.

Ridge knew his father had willed him, Chamridge Westminster, as Arthur and Daisy's guardian. He'd signed the documents of guardianship himself, for he'd insisted his father legalize it, in case they were ever orphaned. Still, there were conditions. In order to claim guardianship of Arthur and Daisy, Ridge would have to claim his father's fortune. If he did not return to claim all the conditions of his father's will, he could not claim Arthur and Daisy. His young siblings would be turned over to appointed guardians—other wealthy aristocrats who would send them into the care of servants.

"I could never abandon them to be raised as heartless, unhappy human beings," Ridge mumbled. "Yet if I journey to claim them, my life here—who I am—would it be lost? Would Ember still love me if I were Chamridge Westminster and not Ridge West?"

Mariner placed a gnarled hand on Ridge's shoulder. "Ya are who ya are, lad," he said. "A good man who would not let a young lad and lass grow up to be what he so struggled to avoid becomin'. That's the man she loves. The name doesn't make the man, lad."

Ridged nodded. "It would take several weeks…in the least," he mumbled, "to have the will read, to instruct the solicitors to sell my father's businesses and properties." His eyes narrowed. "This is who I am—a man who craves a life of hard labor and desperate love. A cottage by the sea is all I ever endeavor to own—one filled with the wife I love to pure obsession, children to hold and bounce on my knee…" He paused, smiling at Mariner. "And portraits of lost sea captains hanging above the hearth."

"Settle your responsibilities, lad," Mariner said, "so that nothing can haunt ya when you're lyin' in Ember's arms in the warm dark of the night. See to your wee siblings' welfare or you'll never have your peace…not even in owning Ember."

Ridge nodded. Though a sense of crushing trepidation washed over him, he knew Mariner was right. He would never know true peace if he abandoned Arthur and Daisy to the life he so loathed. Ember's heart was his, and he knew she would love him more for doing right by his young brother and sister. In truth, he'd never truly considered abandoning them—only kicked against the knowledge he would have to leave Ember in order to journey to save them.

"And what of you, Mariner Taffee?" Ridge asked. "What of the loving wife and daughters waiting for you in the little cottage near Mermaid Cove?"

Mariner's eyes clouded, an obvious fear and sadness smoldering in them. Yet he nodded. "Aye...what of them?" he asked. "I was afraid I would find my Tempest had married another...or given her heart to another man, at least. So I lingered in not revealing myself. The longer I lingered, the more fearful I became that she would despise me for my weakness."

Ridge puffed a breath of disbelief. "To survive being set adrift at sea, over a decade of imprisonment...and obvious physical pain," Ridge said. He shook his head. "What weakness is there in you?"

"Fear," Mariner mumbled. "I am scared—head to toe I am scared. The prison beatings left me thus...and this." He patted his stiff leg.

"But you're alive," Ridge reminded him. "Tempest would care for nothing else—Ember and Lily as well."

Mariner grinned. "Are ya about to tell me that if you can find the courage to brave your father's minions, then I can find enough to stand before the woman I love, battered and worn as I am, and after near fifteen years of abandonment?"

Ridge smiled. "Well, you did not abandon her...but yes." Again he laid a hand on Mariner's shoulder. "If I can brave the bowels of hell that are the influence and power of my father's wealth...then surely you can face one woman."

Mariner smiled. "Apparently you've never, for one moment, been out of Tempest's good graces, lad."

Ridge chuckled. "Not yet. Though the day is young."

Mariner laughed, and again Ridge marveled at how his eyes mimicked his youngest daughter's.

"I should leave at once," Ridge mumbled thoughtfully. "The sooner I leave, the sooner I can return."

"Yes," Mariner said.

"It will worry Ember…my going." Ridge was sick—literally ill. He knew Ember's fears because of the past. Yet he loved her. She had to know that he did. And she would understand. She would want Arthur and Daisy to be cared for properly. He would return to the cottage, explain about his father's death and the danger to Arthur and Daisy. He would ask her to be his wife, and she would say yes. She must say yes! The moment he returned from settling his father's affairs, he would marry his warm, delicious Ember—and with her father's permission.

"She's strong…like her mother," Mariner said. "Ember will weather it. And when ya return, I'll see ya married to her…the very day."

Ridge nodded. It had to be done. He had to leave. In order to ensure he and Ember could bask in the joy their love would afford, he had to ensure that Arthur and Daisy were safe, that his father's wealth was distributed so that there would be no reason for anyone to ever come looking for him again.

Ember tried to breathe—struggled to keep panic at bay.

Ridge's father—dead? His little brother and sister about to be sacrificed on the altar of greed and corruption? She should not be so selfish, so fearful. Yet she was! Indeed, she was terrified.

"How…how long will you be gone?" she asked Ridge.

"Two…maybe three weeks," he answered.

"Three weeks?" Ember breathed. Three weeks? Three weeks— the time it had taken Selkirk to decide to break her heart. Yet Ember struggled to keep the past from haunting her. Ridge must go—he must! He could not leave his little brother and sister to the fates that awaited them if he did not claim their guardianship. Still, Ember trembled, for the dark fear in her whispered, *And if he doesn't return?*

"You know I would take you with me, my pretty mermaid," Ridge told her. "But it's too dangerous. The sailors at the cove are proof of that. I'll never be free…not until my father's fortune can be scattered so that no one on earth cares who or where I am."

"No one…but me?" Ember asked, forcing a smile.

Ridge smiled, yet she saw the conflict in him. "Yes," he said.

Ember let the tears escape her eyes as Ridge rested his head on her lap for a moment. She was sitting on the side of her bed, Ridge kneeling before her, clutching her hands in his near desperately. She feared she might die—literally die in having to release him, in the necessity of allowing him to rescue his siblings. Yet his goodness—his lion's heart—it was part of what made him the rare and powerful man he was. She loved him all the more for his determination, his heroism.

He raised his head and squeezed her hands so tightly in his that it pained her. "When I return," he began, "will you marry me, Ember Taffee?" He looked up into her face. the mesmerizing blue of his eyes pleading with her in desperation. "The moment I return…will you marry me? Will you be mine? Only mine? Thoroughly, wholly, and forever mine?"

Ember couldn't brush the tears from her cheeks, for Ridge yet held her hands. Mustering her last remaining thread of courage, Ember whispered, "Yes! Yes…I'll marry you."

Ridge kissed her hands in his.

"But who will I be?" she asked him, teasing him in an effort to keep from panic.

"What do you mean?" he asked.

"Will I be Ember West? Or Ember Westminster?"

"Legally, you'll be Ember Westminster…wife of the not quite impoverished Chamridge Westminster," he said, smiling.

Ember smiled, pulled her hands from his grasp, and took his face between them. "Hmmm," she began. "I wonder if this Chamridge Westminster will prove to own such an affecting siren's song as you do, son of Neptune." She hoped that teasing him might continue to distract her from her fear and pain. She hoped it would cause him to take her in his arms, to kiss her, for she would have his kiss once more. She would! Before he left for his journey—a journey she knew was well fraught with danger—she would know his loving kiss one last time.

Ridge smiled and stood, pulling her to her feet and into his arms.

"Can't you at least wait until morning to leave?" she asked, brushing a tear from her cheek in sensing this would be the last kiss she would know of him for perhaps weeks—perhaps forever.

"No," he mumbled as he began to unbutton the buttons at the collar and front of her blouse.

"But why not?" she asked, gasping as she felt his lips press the hollow of her throat—as she felt him unfasten three more buttons at the front of her blouse.

"Because I love you," he mumbled, pressing a kiss to her flesh just below the place he'd kissed before. He placed a strong, gentle palm to the space above her bosom. "This heart beating in you—the one you call your own—in truth, it belongs to me. And I mean to safeguard it, protect it from harm, as I mean to protect you from harm—whether it be heartbreak, danger, or villains in search of wealth…or whether it's the villain in *me* wanting to seize you here and now…regardless of your mother's and sister's presence in the other room." He paused, smiling and adding, "Or that contemptible creature in the painting above your mantel."

Ember covered his hand that pressed to her heart.

"Then go," she wept. "Go. Do what you must. Only promise me that…"

His promise was his kiss—his hot, driven, demanding passion's kiss!

Ember gasped once for air, but he did not let her breathe long, claiming her mouth with his own—claiming her heart, her body, her very soul! Instantly, she was lost—carried away on warm waves of wanting, bathing in pools of desire, in an ocean of truest love.

He broke from her suddenly, his breathing labored. "Arrange it, Ember. Whatever is necessary…the means of our union, Ember," he nearly growled. "For you *will* marry me the moment I return! I won't wait an instant beyond it." He kissed her again—ravenous—careless of the fact her mother and sister had entered the room. "I love you," he whispered, his lips pressed firm against her ear.

"I love you," she sobbed, tears streaming down her cheeks.

He released her, and she felt as if she might crumble to dust.

Turning, Ridge strode to the door. He paused, cupping Lily's cheek affectionately as he shook his head, nodding toward the painting over Ember's mantel. "I forgive you for that, little sister," he chuckled.

Lily smiled, bit her lip, and nodded.

He turned to Tempest then. "I've left something of great value in the cove, Tempest Taffee…near the Dirk and his mermaid," he said. "At sunset, please retrieve it for me."

"Of course, darling," Tempest said, returning Ridge's loving embrace.

He looked to Ember, and her heart leapt.

"I will come back to you, Ember," he said. "I will come back, and then you won't be able to keep me from…" He paused, glanced to Tempest, and grinned. "Then nothing will keep me from you…from owning you as my wife."

Ridge was gone, and it seemed the very air was somehow tainted without him. Ember wept—trembled—feared—forced herself to hope. Ridge loved her! He did! And he would return and love her still! As her hands began to tremble—as Lily embraced her with comforting love—Ember tried to think of Arthur and Daisy, of the misery Ridge had known as a child. She would never have contemplated his abandoning them, and yet her heart ached with remembered heartache—with thoughts of Selkirk Beacon, of even her own father being lost at sea. She could not endure losing Ridge—not in any manner.

"He loves you, Ember," Lily whispered. "You have no need to fear."

"God will protect him, darling," Tempest said. "Only pray, and God will see him safely back to you."

Ember nodded, though she thought of her own father. Her mother knew her well, however.

"This is your story, Ember," Tempest said. "God will protect your Ridge for you."

Ember wondered if her mother still felt her husband had been taken for the sake of his wife's imperfections. She knew that—no matter the forgiveness Mariner Taffee, Lily, Ember, and even God had given Tempest—her mother had never forgiven herself for her transgressions and failings.

Somehow, Ember sensed her mother needed strength in that moment. Ember's father had been lost. Ember knew her mother loved her and Lily more than her own life, that her mother's fear must be nearly as great as Ember's own, for she would not want to see Ember in pain. Thus, for the sake of her mother—and the sake of her love for Ridge—Ember drew a deep breath.

"He will come back to me," Ember whispered. "And when he does…he'll love me still." She sat down on her bed, feeling lightheaded even for her determination to remain strong. "He's…he's Chamridge Westminster, you know, Lily," Ember whispered. Neither Ember nor Ridge had explained to Tempest or Lily why it was Ridge needed to journey away for so long. There hadn't been time when Ridge had first returned from town.

"Chamridge Westminster?" Lily repeated. "Westminster? I heard of a Westminster that died of recent…a wealthy man who…"

"Ridge is Arthur Westminster's missing heir?" Tempest asked.

Ember nodded. "Yes," she breathed. "And we'll never be free, not until the children are safe and his father's estates are sold."

Lily frowned. "Ember, what are you talking about?"

"I'll tell you," Ember began, "though it sounds like some story from a book." She paused, gazing up at the painting of the merman in the bottle. "Or some myth or fairy tale Father might have told us as children."

Mariner gazed out to the horizon. The sun was beginning its descent into the sea. Soon only the moon and stars would light the darkness. He fancied the moon would be full—thought of the stories he used to tell Ember concerning mermaids and their gift to come ashore when the moon was full round. Battling the bitter resentment that began to well in him—for he had missed their growing-up years, Lily's and Ember's—Mariner thought only of the future.

His body was battered, scarred, and broken from the beatings and neglect over a decade in prison had inflicted on him. But he was a free man now, and Tempest was a free woman. He'd lingered in town long enough to know she had not accepted the attentions of any man who offered them. It was said that Tempest Taffee's heart wandered the bottom of the sea in company with her husband. The residents of Trident Point spoke of nothing but good where Tempest and her daughters were concerned. It seemed that even the arrival of the stranger, Ridge West, had not given rise to gossip. The townsfolk seemed to think that Tempest and her daughters could do no wrong—and Mariner was glad of it.

Still, he doubted. He'd seen himself in the mirror of Ridge's room. Certainly, his own well-fitting clothes—the clothes Ridge had discarded for more appropriate ones of his own—refined his appearance, as did the haircut and shaving Ridge and he had managed. He'd bathed, of course, though quickly. Yet the vision of himself in the inn mirror—leather-skinned, scarred, lame—what man could hope that such a woman as Tempest would see beyond the battered body of an old sailor to the soul and heart that had never stopped loving her?

He heard Tempest then—heard her singing as she wandered the path leading to the cove's shore. He smiled, recognizing the melody she sang as one of his favorites—one he used to sing to Lily and Ember when tucking them snuggly into their beds so many years before. His muscles tensed. Would she reject him? Would she loathe and despise him for abandoning her and their beloved daughters?

"Hello!" she called. "It is a lovely night for searching for treasures on the shore, isn't it?"

Mariner did not turn, nor did he answer. Fear had frozen him—fear of rejection, heartbreak, and pain.

"I've come at Ridge West's bidding," she began. "He said he left something here, and I'm to retrieve it. Do you happen to know, sir, what the boy…"

Her voice trailed. Mariner was certain she'd recognized his clothes. After all, hadn't she given them to the lad herself a short time before?

"I would've returned to ya sooner, lass," Mariner said, "if I'd been able." He swallowed the lump of fear in his throat and turned to face his love.

Tempest's breath caught in her throat. She thought certain she was dreaming—for she could not be awake! Thus, she surmised she was either dreaming—or dead! So many times she'd dreamt of Mariner's return; so many times she'd awaken in tears, knowing he would ever only return in her dreams. Yet she could feel the spray of the sea on her face, taste the salt of it. She could hear the call of the evening birds, the soft music of the calm surf, and she knew she wasn't asleep.

"I must be dead," she whispered—for what else could explain the presence of Mariner Taffee on the shore of Mermaid Cove? Tempest knew she had died, and she was glad of it, for it was Mariner who was waiting in heaven to greet her!

"The pirates could have slaughtered us, Tempest," Mariner began, "but they didn't. They put us adrift, and we were found…taken to Barbados…imprisoned. I rotted in prison for over twelve years, Tempest—rotted and dreamt of nothin' but this moment."

Tempest couldn't breathe! She gasped, knowing by the mingling pain and joy in her heart that she was neither dead nor dreaming.

"Two years I spent in fightin' my way back to ya, lass," he said. "And now…I stand here before ya—battered, broken, worthless to all the world…and yet hopin' that…"

Mariner gasped as the beautiful woman flew into his arms, laughing with joy, sobbing with disbelief and muttered prayers of thanks, kissing his weathered cheeks.

"Tempest," he breathed, finding her mouth with his own.

Her kiss—the familiar warmth of her mouth—in that moment, Mariner was whole once more! He felt as if God himself had breathed life into him. There would be time for explanation, or so his soul whispered to his mind. But in that moment, as Mariner felt his heart swelling—felt a strength in his body he hadn't known in near fifteen years—he gathered Tempest into his arms, drawing power and passion from her tender lips. In that moment, it was as if they'd never been apart, as if all the pain and loneliness, the torture and uncertain hope, had vanished—near never existed.

"Mariner!" Tempest sobbed as he broke the seal of their kiss to hold her to him. "Oh, Mariner, my darling!" She felt her knees buckle—felt her husband catch her, lay her back gently in the sand. She couldn't lose consciousness. She couldn't! She might wake to find him gone again. Thus, Tempest fought to keep hold of her senses.

"Mariner," she whispered, placing a trembling palm to his cheek as he hovered just above her. There were scars on his face, scars he had not borne before. She let her fingers caress them—the one at the corner of his mouth, the one at his forehead. She buried her hands in his black and silver hair, smiling, for it became him, even more than it had when it had been full ebony.

"Mariner," she whispered again.

"Tempest," he said—and she wept at the sound of his voice. Throwing her weak and trembling arms around his neck, she pulled him to her—kissed him with years of missing him, years of constant yearning and missing him.

Mariner did not pause but rather drew her against him, his mouth working the same bewitching spell of passion over her it ever had. Tempest was blissful—euphoric in the sense of his touch.

Suddenly she was aware of where they were—in Mermaid Cove, just beneath the stone structure of the Dirk and the Mermaid. Yet it was not the pain of mistakes in her past that entered her mind—no. Rather it was the legend of the Dirk of Fortune and Cordelia—lovers forever embracing, forever entwined in passion and love. Tempest Taffee knew there would be no greater curse—no, no greater blessing—than to be as the Dirk of Fortune and his Cordelia, forever entwined, forever touching, never to be parted again.

A freedom and hope her heart had not known since she was a child breathed into her as she embraced her husband, as he kissed her, held her, and loved her there.

"Mariner," she breathed.

He paused in administering his attentions. "Tempest," he said.

"I love you," she whispered.

She saw the tears in his dark eyes—his eyes that were as dark and as diamond-dusted as the moonlit sky above them, the star-sifted moonlit sky.

"I love you, Tempest Taffee," he said. "Will ya have me back, lass?" he asked.

He brushed the tears from her temples as she nodded and breathed, "Yes! Did you ever doubt it?"

He winced, and her heart ached in knowing he had.

"Well, if you'll have me…then let the Dirk and his mermaid blush," he mumbled, "for I mean to quench me thirst for ya here and now."

As Mariner's mouth claimed her own, Tempest Taffee wept—wept for the miracle of mercy and love. She cared nothing for the sea spray misting over them—disregarded the loud crack, the sound of slowly splitting rock. Lost in the paradise of passion, neither Tempest nor Mariner noticed that the Dirk and the Mermaid, still standing as sentinels over them, now bore another deep fracture. In that moment, there were only Mariner and Tempest—wife and husband—lovers—blissfully reunited.

CHAPTER ELEVEN
TREASURES OF THE TIDE

Four weeks had closed since Ridge had gone—four weeks, not two, not three. Four weeks since Ember's father had miraculously returned. Four weeks since the legendary rock, the Dirk and the Mermaid, had disappeared during the night, leaving only a trail of crumbled rock and mermaid tears strewn over the sand of Mermaid Cove.

Ember had been to the cove that morning, searching the shore for any residual tears of joy Cordelia and her sisters had left behind when Neptune took the Dirk and his lover into the sea. She'd found five, amazed that she'd found any at all. Yet she had found them, just as she had every morning for the past four weeks. The bottles on the mantel filled with the tears of Cordelia and her sisters numbered five, each filled with the beautiful sea glass left in the cove when the rock had crumbled. Ember's father surmised that eons of tides had collected the horde of mermaid tears into the crevices and crannies of Mermaid Rock. When the rock had cracked and crumbled, the sea glass multitude had spilled out onto the sand as a bright and brilliant treasure. Ember and Lily had delighted in collecting the mermaid tears. Many were ancient and worn perfectly round like marbles.

Furthermore, Ember knew what had broken the rock—what had stripped the stone from the Dirk of Fortune and Cordelia and freed them. True love had been thrice presented before them. The first true love presented had been that shared by a young Tempest and her Seward—Lily's father. Tragic though the story was, Tempest had desperately loved Seward, as he had her. The third true love presented had been her own father returning after over a decade of imprisonment and misery to find that he yet owned her mother's heart as desperately as ever he had. Furthermore, Ember knew the second true love presented before the Dirk and the Mermaid had been she and Ridge, the day Ridge had saved her from being taken by the sailors—the day he'd also saved her from drowning, the day he'd carried her to the shore beneath the Dirk and the Mermaid and loved her so truly as to champion her virtue instead of pressing her to sacrifice it, or allowing her to. Thus, she knew that thrice true love had been presented before the Dirk and the Mermaid, that the Fates had been bested, that Neptune had taken his most beautiful mermaid and her pirate lover back to the sea to dwell forever in their own love.

Oh, certainly it was all fancy, myth, and fairy tale. Yet Ember delighted in imagining that the Dirk and Cordelia were truly together at last. Further, it gave her hope, when hope was quickly fleeting. Ridge loved her; she was certain he did. He would return to her—he would! She knew it!

There had been no word from Ridge. He'd told Ember before he'd left to champion little Arthur and Daisy that he would be unable to contact her—that it would not be safe to do so. Correspondence was easily traced, and Ridge knew that his father's death would draw out those wanting to somehow own a part of his father's great fortune. He'd reminded her of the four sailors from the Wayward Maiden, how they'd meant to take her. There were others that would attempt ransom—either of Ember and her family or of little Arthur and Daisy. Therefore, Ridge had neither written nor sent a telegram. The only assurance Ember had of even his safety was a cryptic letter received by Lily from a solicitor named Reginald Oakley two weeks before.

As Ember walked along the shore, meandering from the cove down the seaside to the very place she'd first found Ridge that morning seeming so long ago, she thought of the solicitor's letter to Lily. She'd memorized it, of course, for it was her only shred of tangible proof that Ridge was alive and well—or at least, had been alive and well.

"Dear Miss Taffee," Ember breathed, reciting the words of the letter aloud as she walked. *"Please rest assured that we are in receipt of your work, The Merman in the Bottle. The painting arrived at the auction house in perfect condition. There is not a marring mark upon it, and we assure it will draw a pretty price. The Merman in the Bottle is being kept in an undisclosed location now as we make preparations for its sale. We are still awaiting the arrival of the two smaller paintings you mentioned—one entitled The Little White Flower and the other Camelot's Boy King. We are anxious to receive them as well and will place them in safe storage with their larger counterpart work as soon as they arrive. I will personally deliver the sum of your earnings to you when the paintings have been sold. As your solicitor, I encourage you to know that your paintings will be cared for. Though it may take longer than originally anticipated for their sale, all will be well, and you will one day bask in the freedom born of your artful patience. Respectfully Yours, Reginald Oakley, Solicitor."*

Ember drew a deep breath and attempted to calm her anxieties. Ridge loved her. She reminded herself that he did. Nearly every moment of every day she silently reminded herself of the smoldering quality of his eyes as he'd looked at her—of the delicious passion evident in his kiss. She listened to the memories of his voice in her mind, heard him saying the words to her—promising to return, demanding she marry him when he did.

Desperate for distraction, for her head ached with the effort of keeping doubt and fear at bay, Ember tried to think of other things—of other people. She thought of her father, smiling as she remembered the astonishment and overwhelming joy that had washed over her and Lily when her mother had returned from the shore some time after sunset on the day Ridge left. Her mother had entered the cottage with a man—a man who Ember recognized at once as her father! She'd scolded herself for having seen him before, for not having recognized him. Though her father had been ragged and bearded, Ember was angry at herself for not having at once recognized his soul! Yet her father had reminded her that Ridge had been with her when they'd met before and that when one is in the presence of her true love, nothing else is recognizable. Ember had taken little comfort in his assurances, yet she had found great comfort and joy in his embrace. Her father had returned! Had it not been for her fears for Ridge's sake, for her loneliness at his lack of company, Ember would have been perfectly content and happy in that first moment of her father's return. Still, she wondered how she would have endured Ridge's absence had her father not been with them.

Mariner Taffee was yet strong, even for his stiff leg and scarred body. Ember rejoiced in her mother's beaming countenance—the love she saw plain between Mariner and Tempest. Often they would disappear for hours on end, returning with smiles of pure joy, passion, and contentment on their faces. When they were not disappeared to some private place, they were in conversation, either with each other or with their daughters. For this reason, the past four weeks since her father's return had not found Ember alone for more than a short time during the day. She was glad of this, for her family helped her to remain strong, faithful that Ridge would be protected—and that he would return. She did not think of Selkirk or worry that Ridge would find another love, for her soul knew that he loved her as full desperately as she loved him. She only worried for his safety, awash in unwavering and painful agony in longing for his return.

Ember gasped then, astonished and delighted as her gaze saw something protruding from the sand. Smiling, she knelt and carefully brushed away sand and kelp clinging to the two halves of beautiful angel wing shells! She giggled, enchanted at having found two halves to the same clam. As she gently pulled them from the sand, she surmised they were nearly six inches in length.

"Beautiful!" she breathed. "How pretty!"

"What did you find, lady?"

Startled at the sudden realization she was not alone on the shore, Ember glanced back to see a little tousle-haired boy standing behind her. He was a towheaded little fellow with bright green eyes, freckles sprinkled across his nose and cheeks, and two front teeth missing.

He wore no shoes or shirt—only a pair of brown trousers rolled up to his knees. She thought he might not have bothered rolling them up, for they were soaking wet to his waist.

"Angel wings," Ember said, holding the shells toward him. "They're very rare. At least finding two together is rare."

"They're nice," the boy said. He looked to Ember, squinting one eye. "Are you a mermaid?" he asked. "They told us in town that there was a mermaid loose around these parts. A pirate too. I'd rather see the pirate, but a mermaid will do."

Ember giggled. The disappearance of the Dirk and the Mermaid had kept the Trident Point townsfolk talking for weeks. She surmised the boy had been privy to the legends and stories.

"Well, I'm not a mermaid," Ember said.

"She's not the mermaid!" the boy called over his shoulder.

"Oh, but she looks like a mermaid!' a little fair-haired girl giggled, splashing in the tide along the shore as she ran to stand beside the boy. The little girl looked as near to an angel from heaven as any child Ember had ever seen! Her eyes too were green, and she also had a large empty space where two front teeth had once resided. She wore only bloomers and a camisole, having obviously discarded her petticoats and dress somewhere.

"I don't know you," Ember said. "Do I know your parents? Or are you visitors to Trident Point?" Ember looked up and down the shore, but she saw no adults that the children might belong to.

"We live here now!" the angelic girl chimed. "But we don't have any parents...not anymore."

"Oh, I'm so sorry," Ember said. Still, as the little girl smiled up at her, an odd sense of understanding began to wash over her. Her heart began to hammer inside her chest. She couldn't breathe!

"But we have a brother," the little boy offered cheerfully. He took the angel wing shells from Ember's hand and placed his in her grasp, just as the little girl took hold of her other hand. Gently they tugged at her until she bent closer to them.

"And don't tell anyone," the boy whispered.

"But our brother is a merman," the girl finished.

"What?" Ember gasped, her heart nearly bursting from her bosom for its violent pounding.

"It's true!" the boy whispered. "Look there…just there," he said, pointing to the sea. "Look there, and you'll see!"

Trembling—unable to draw a steady breath—Ember looked to the sea. She saw nothing at first, her heart near breaking for the emptiness of the water. But then—then she gasped, tears flooding her cheeks as, of a sudden, Ridge's head broke the surface of the water. Ember shook her head, afraid to believe it as she watched him slowly rise from the waves like some mythical creature of the sea. First his broad shoulders broke the surface, then his muscular arms and torso, until at last he was walking toward her, wearing only his trousers and looking exactly as he'd looked the day she'd first found him washed ashore.

She didn't wait for him to walk to the shore but rather dropped the children's hands and ran to meet him. In the next moment, they were tumbling into the shallows—desperate in their embracing, ravenous in their kiss! Ember trembled and wept as the heat of Ridge's mouth demanded the moisture of hers. She thrilled at the sound of the low chuckle in his throat—shuddered at the knowledge he had returned to her.

"Ember," he breathed, gazing into her eyes as they lay in the sand and the softly lapping waves on the shore. "I love you. Oh, how desperately I love you! I thought I would die from wanting you in my arms!"

He held her to him as she whispered her own words of love in his ear—as she wept with joy!

"You're all wet now, pretty mermaid," the little towheaded girl said.

Ember opened her eyes, brushed tears from her cheeks, and saw Daisy leaning over her. Arthur was at her side, his hands placed firmly on his knees as he smiled at her.

"I'm Artie, and this is Daisy," he said. "And you're even prettier than Chamridge said you were!"

"Yes!" Daisy giggled. "You are as pretty as a mermaid!"

Ember looked to Ridge, took his ethereal handsome face between her hands, and kissed him. He did not pause in claiming her mouth with a famished fervor!

"Mr. Reggie! Mr. Reggie!" she heard Artie call over his shoulder. "Did you bring them? Did you bring the clergyman and everyone else?"

Ember glanced to see her mother, father, and Lily approaching. Reverend Crossin was with them and a young man Ember did not recognize.

"Yes, Artie," the stranger said. "I've brought them all."

Ember smiled as Ridge kissed the tears from her cheeks.

"You promised," he said, smiling at her, tears of love and joy brimming in his own eyes. "You promised you'd marry me the minute I returned."

"I did...and I will," she whispered.

Ridge sighed, as if he'd been half afraid she'd refuse him.

He wiped a tear from her temple and kissed the tip of her nose. "We're free, Ember," he said. "We're free...all of us. My father's businesses and properties...sold, gone, liquidated, and hidden in trusts for the twins, Reggie, and us. As far as the wealthy world knows, Chamridge Westminster is of no consequence."

"Chamridge Westminster," Ember breathed, gazing into the inviting blue seas of his eyes. "He is of infinite consequence to me."

Ridge smiled, kissed her hard, and then pushed himself from her and lifted her to her feet. "Will you marry me here...now?" he asked. "Without delay, Ember...my pretty Ember mermaid? I know it's no grand cathedral."

"Isn't it?" Ember asked, glancing up into a brilliant blue sky, nodding toward the sea.

Ridge grasped Ember's hands in his own, drew them to his lips, and kissed them. "I asked your mother's permission to marry you before I left...and your father's," he said. He looked to Reverend Crossin and demanded, "Marry us...now."

"A poet?" Ember giggled, allowing her hand to caress the warm contours of Ridge's broad chest. "He's given up solicitation for writing poetry?"

In truth, she was little interested in Reginald Oakley or his changed career in that moment. She wanted only to linger in the strong, protective, loving arms of her husband. Still, she did think of the prophecy her father had made to Lily when she was a child—that Ember was meant to love a merman and Lily a poet. Oh, surely she knew her father had been teasing young Lily. Yet now—now she wondered. For here she lay in the loving arms of Ridge, who had come to her from the sea.

Ember smiled and kissed Ridge's shoulder—snuggled closer to him as he tucked the blanket of their bed at her back.

Ridge smiled and chuckled as he caught Ember's gentle hand and drew it to his lips. How he loved the feel of her in his arms—the warmth of her body lying next to his.

"Yes," he admitted. "Reggie always hated being a solicitor…though he proved to be very good at it. Still, he detested it. He used to say the only joy he derived from the profession came through the documents he penned—the use of words, manipulating verbiage until it sounded as close to legal poetry as he could summon." He smiled, remembering the expression he'd seen plain on Reggie's face when first his friend had set eyes upon Lily— remembering the light that had flamed in Lily's eyes for Reggie's sake.

Ember sighed and kissed his cheek. "Lily will love him," she said.

Ridge chuckled again. "And he'll love her. You should've seen his face when he saw the painting of that ridiculous merman. 'Remarkable!' he exclaimed…as if it were to put da Vinci's *Mona Lisa* to shame!" He laughed and hugged his wife to him.

The fire burned warm in the small hearth of the bedroom in the little cottage by the sea. Outside Ember could hear the soft whisper of the sea as it lapped to shore. Ember wondered that Reginald had been able to secure the old property so quickly for Ridge's sake—as his wedding gift to her.

She'd always been intrigued by the small, abandoned cottage known as the Dirk's Haven by the townsfolk of Trident—the few who cared to remember it existed. Located nearly a mile downshore from Taffee Cottage, the Dirk's Haven was nestled on a hillside overlooking a stretch of sandy seaside little visited by beachcombers and townsfolk for the rocks surrounding it. Ridge had asked Reggie to do him one last favor as his solicitor—to hire several women and men who mended and prepared the cottage just before Ridge was to return. Thus, the cottage was warm and clean, well stocked with supplies, and isolated—the perfect haven for newlywed lovers.

Ridge turned his head, smiled at her, and claimed her mouth in a slow, nearly weary sort of kiss. Already Ridge was resenting the coming sunrise. Ember had been his—all the night long she'd been his—and though he knew he would still own her in the light of the dawning day, he silently wished for the night—that the very moment would never end.

He brushed a strand of hair from her cheek, kissed her forehead, and she smiled.

"Father and Mother may steal the twins from us, you know," she said. "Both Artie and Daisy seem quite taken with them." She sighed, adding, "And Mother is already nesting about. It seems to me the beds she prepared for them in the spare room had an all-too-permanent appearance."

"Your father already asked me if he and your mother could parent them," Ridge confessed then. "And I agreed."

"You did?" she asked, raising herself on one elbow to look at him.

Ridge nodded. "We'll be right here, close by, and after all, I do think Tempest and Mariner Taffee to be the greatest mother and father ever to walk the earth. I couldn't hope for better for Artie and Daisy. Are you angry with me, for letting the twins go to them?"

She smiled, her palm warm and invigorating as she pressed it to his chest. "No," she whispered, placing a light kiss to his wanting lips. "I confess to wanting you all to myself for a while."

"Do you?" he teased. "Why?"

"Because I'm selfish," she breathed, kissing him again. "The tide once washed a treasure to the shore, and since I can't keep it in a bottle on a shelf, I intend to keep it here...in my arms."

Ridge smiled, his strength suddenly rejuvenated for the sake of his loving want. Gently yet boldly, he aggressed, taking Ember in his arms, shifting his weight so that he hovered over her dominantly.

Ember smiled, weaving her fingers through Ridge's soft, dark hair.

"I love you, my pretty mermaid," he breathed a moment before his mouth demanded hers respond to him.

"I love you," Ember breathed between impassioned kisses, "my beloved treasure of the sea."

And the tide's soft caress kissed the moonlit shore...

And now, enjoy the first chapter of
MIDNIGHT MASQUERADE
by Marcia Lynn McClure.

CHAPTER ONE

She was tired—oh, so very, very tired. Never, not in all her life, had Evony Elorietta known such thoroughgoing fatigue. As she trudged out of the dark woods still veiled in the shadows of early sunrise, out across the expanse of cold, dew-drenched grass, and onto the main road of the village, Evony wondered how she would ever endure a day that was only just beginning. Every bone in her body ached; every muscle throbbed in misery; every inch of her flesh begged for respite. Yet there would be none—at least not until she had finished her stitching—finished the near thirteen hours of sewing she now faced under the ever-observant, incessantly critical eye of seamstress Agnes Teche.

After such a long, chilled, and sleepless night spent in watching, peering through the darkness and into the rooms of the inn in the woods until her eyes were too dry to watch any longer—after listening to the shallow, often vile conversations until her ears hurt from the foul ferment of it—Evony dreaded sewing for Mrs. Teche more than ever before. The woman was a banshee of an employer. And yet she was grateful Mrs. Teche had had the keen eye to recognize Evony's superior skills with needle and thread—for how else would Evony have managed to feed Mikol and Tressa, to shelter them, to keep them hidden?

Certainly she was not able to feed her young brother and sister *well*. In truth, many nights found only enough coin in Evony's pocket for the price of three potatoes or half a dozen eggs. Yet food was food, whether or not it was scant and plain to the palate. And as for their shelter—indeed, there were larger hovels to be had but none so insignificant, and thereby less perceptible, than the one Miss Lovie had helped Evony to procure. The small dwelling kept Mikol and Tressa warm and hidden, and it was comfortable enough. Thus, Evony was thankful for it—thankful for Miss Lovie and the measure of safety they all knew there.

Evony sighed, wondering what in all the world would have become of Mikol, Tressa, and herself had they not been inadvertently discovered by Miss Lovie that day in the outer courtyard of Abawyth Castle. What would have been their collective fates if not for the kindness of a stranger? Would they have "disappeared" as their mother had? Yet in her soul, Evony knew their consequences would have been nothing less than dark, secret imprisonment deep within the castle's bowels—especially for Mikol.

Hence, not a day had passed since in which Evony did not graciously and sincerely express gratitude to the diminutive, sweet old woman, Lovie Wiggin, for her benevolent charity. Tenderhearted, aged, and bent with long years of work that was too hard, Miss Lovie was no less than a guardian angel. Even now, as Evony stepped onto the muddy main street of the village, she could see Lovie making her own way to meet her. No doubt Mikol and Tressa had begun to worry about their elder sister and begged Lovie to go in search of Evony. She smiled as Miss Lovie tossed a wave to her and quickened her step.

As the comforting aroma of baking breads and pastries wafted from the baker's shop to weave an invisible veil over the alleyways and streets of the village, Evony's stomach moaned with hunger. If she hurried, she would have just enough time to purchase food for breakfast, return home to cook for the children, and perhaps freshen herself a bit before hurrying to Mrs. Teche's.

"Good morning, Simon," Evony greeted the young boy holding a basket of fresh eggs as he stepped in front of her.

"Good morning to you, miss," Simon responded with a smile and a nod. "It's eggs for breakfast today then, miss?" he asked.

"Yes, Simon," Evony answered, smiling. Simon was younger than Mikol's ten years. She fancied he was perhaps just older than Tressa's six years. Yet he often spoke with the manner of a matured man and sold his mother's eggs with admirable determination.

"The usual number, miss?" Simon asked.

"Yes. Six."

Evony watched as Simon selected the six largest eggs in his basket. "Be watchful, miss. We wouldn't want them breaking and robbing you of your meal this morning, now would we?"

"Indeed not," Evony giggled, pleased by sweet Simon's concern and amused by the adult intonation of his voice. Carefully placing the eggs in her front apron pocket, Evony pressed a coin into Simon's outstretched hand and said, "Thank you, Simon. I hope you fare well today."

"As I hope you do, miss," Simon said with a lingering, pleased smile.

As Simon hurried off in search of others in want of his fare, Miss Lovie arrived, breathlessly announcing, "Oh, Evony! Another man has failed." Shaking her white-haired head with distress, she continued, "That brave young lord from Pariveth. The strange stupor of the castle claimed him each of these past four days, and this morning when he woke…the king dismissed him."

"Of course the king dismissed him," Evony grumbled. "The king is waiting for a man to arrive far wealthier than the young lord of Pariveth." Lowering her voice as she noted Simon glancing back to her, Evony added, "Or the even greater possibility to my mind is that the king does not want the mystery solved."

Lovie nodded. "As long as the princesses are kept weak and overcome with fatigue so much of the time, no one in the kingdom will question King Standwood's sitting the throne of Abawyth."

"Just as no one will question the steward he placed in Elawyth," Evony added. She shook her head. "Great fatigue, blistered heels, and puffy eyes," she sighed. "Why is it all that any physician can determine is wrong with the princesses? Any subject of this kingdom could determine that."

Lovie again shook her head. "And it does no good that each physician called upon bleeds them nearly dry with leeches."

"Bleeds them with leeches?" Simon exclaimed, suddenly appearing at Evony's side.

Evony forced a smile and tousled Simon's straw-colored hair. "Oh, do not worry, Simon," she fibbed to soothe him. "Miss Lovie and I are only making up stories with which to entertain ourselves."

"So the princesses will be healed…even though no physician can explain their blistered feet and weary ways?" Simon asked, looking to Lovie hopefully.

"Of course," Lovie reassured. "If no physician can heal them, then love will." Lovie smiled at the boy. "It is just why King Standwood has called for suitors for the princesses…called for champions to come from far and near, to endeavor to solve the mystery of our sleepy princesses. Somewhere there is a man from a kingdom who will triumph over whatever plagues our twelve princesses of Abawyth with weariness."

"Good," Simon sighed. "We are yet mourning the loss of our dear queen. What despair would fall upon the people if the princesses were lost?"

"Yes," Lovie agreed. "What despair indeed?"

A church bell echoing in the distance drew Evony's attention back to the tasks before her. "Oh! I must hurry, Miss Lovie…lest my dear ones go hungry all the day long."

Realizing that the sun had risen far higher in the east than she had realized, Evony retrieved the eggs from her apron pocket in favor of cradling them in her hands to ensure they did not jostle together and become cracked.

"I must hurry," she mumbled to herself as she darted into the street toward home.

"Evony!" she heard Miss Lovie cry out, an instant before the surprised whinny of a horse echoed—an instant before she turned and looked up to see an enormous black gelding rearing just before her.

Screaming with the realization she was about to be trampled, Evony leapt backward. An immediate and sharp pain stabbed her ankle. She tumbled to the muddy street, barely escaping the horse's powerful hooves as they slammed into the ground before her.

Even for the pain in her ankle and the mud that now covered the seat of her skirt, it was the sight of the broken eggs lying next to her on the ground that brought tears to Evony's eyes—for she had not one more coin with which to purchase others. Her young brother and sister would go hungry until Mrs. Teche paid wages to Evony when she'd finished her work that evening.

"Whoa there, Bromius!" a deep voice ordered as the horse stomped twice at the ground before Evony.

Evony heard the rider's heavy boots hit the mud as he dismounted—heard his deep, commanding voice ask, "Are you injured, miss?"

But she could not answer. She could not move but instead only stare at the shattered eggs seeping into the mud next to her.

"Evony!" Miss Lovie cried as she knelt beside her. "Are you hurt, my darling?"

At last Evony was able to pull her stare from the miserable sight of the wasted eggs to look at her friend. "They'll be so hungry, Miss Lovie," she muttered as tears escaped her eyes to begin streaming over her cheeks.

"You have my sincerest apologies, miss," the rider's voice offered. "You were so quick into the street that I could not rein him any faster. I truly feared Bromius would trample you…however unintentionally."

At last Evony looked up to the man. Instantly her long-withheld tears of fear and fatigue and frustration increased to profusion—for she knew at once why the man had come to Abawyth, and it inexplicably pained her heart.

It was obvious he was a noble—a lord, perhaps. It might be he was even a royal, a prince of some kingdom, come to solve the mystery of the princesses of Abawyth—to claim the hand of one of the twelve princesses in marriage as reward. Dressed as a man of wealth and title, from his black boots of the finest leather to the heavy fur cape he wore, the man's bearing was intimidating—and wildly affecting. Yet it was not so much his manner of dress and bearing that spoke to Evony of his importance and power, but rather the perfect comeliness of his features and face. He was, by any measure, the most handsome of men—broad-shouldered, square-jawed, blue-eyed, black-haired, and entrancingly attractive in every means in which a man could be attractive.

"You've come to win the hand of a princess of Abawyth," Evony remarked.

Yet the man seemed not to hear her—or chose to ignore her statement—for he simply asked, "Are you injured, miss?"

"No," Evony answered as the man took hold of her arm, placed one of his own around her waist, and began to assist her to stand. Yet the instant Evony attempted to bear her own weight, the sharp pain in her ankle dreadfully reminded her that she had indeed been injured. "Ow!" she gasped, wincing.

"You *have* been injured," the man growled, frowning.

"No, no," Evony argued. "I only twisted an ankle. I am well enough, sire." Of a sudden, Evony remembered Mrs. Teche and her sewing. "And I must hurry, lest I be tardy and lose my position with the seamstress."

"You will not be laboring for your seamstress today," the man stated, effortlessly lifting Evony into the cradle of his powerful arms.

"Oh, but I must!" Evony cried in desperation. Wiping tears from her cheeks, she added, "I will lose my position if I do not work even one hour of what I am meant to. And I do not need two good ankles in order to stitch and sew well."

"It is true, sire," Lovie ventured to the man. "Agnes Teche will not hold the girl's position...not even for reasons of illness or injury."

The man's frown deepened, and he said to Lovie, "I will see to it myself that this young woman does not lose her position with the seamstress." He looked to Evony then, and she found that the stunning blue of his eyes caused her tears to increase once more for some reason she could not fathom. "I nearly cost you your life, miss," the man explained. "I will certainly see to it that I do not cost you your employment with this Agnes Teche." He paused a moment, glancing down at the broken eggs lying in the mud. "And I will make recompense for your loss there, as well."

"Oh no, no, no! Please!" Evony argued. "I have no desire to be indebted to you, sire."

Again the frown furrowing his handsome brown increased. "You? Indebted to me?" The man looked to Lovie inquisitively and then back to Evony. "My horse nearly trampled you, miss. He and I robbed you of not only your breakfast and a day's wage but nearly your life. Why would you think yourself indebted to me for making whatever recompense that I am able?"

But as Evony could only linger speechless in the man's strong arms—bathe in the unfamiliar warmth emanated by his body and the furs he wore—Lovie answered, "She is near feverish with fatigue, sire," Lovie said. "Not a wink of sleep during the night and looking to a full day of stitching ahead of her."

"Miss Lovie!" Evony quietly scolded. "I am full well enough and—"

"Where is this seamstress…this Agnes Teche?" the man interrupted, glancing around him to the village shops lining the street. "Surely when I explain the situation, Agnes Teche will be understanding and compliant."

"She is just there," Lovie said as she gestured toward Agnes's shop. "She is the one of the queen's favorite seamstresses." Pausing, Lovie added, "Well, she *was* one of the queen's favorite seamstresses."

"Come then, miss," the man ordered as he began striding toward the shop, still carrying Evony in his arms. "Bromius! Follow," he commanded his horse.

"Sire, please," Evony began to plead, "I promise you that Mrs. Teche will show me no mercy. Please put me down and allow me to go my way."

"Nonsense," the man grumbled. "She will not be so callous once she has seen how injured you are."

Evony glanced over the man's broad shoulder to Lovie as she followed them. Yet Lovie only shrugged aged shoulders and shook her head with uncertainty.

Without hesitation, the man pushed the door of the seamstress's shop open with one booted foot. Stepping into the main room, he called, "I am looking for Agnes Teche."

But Evony had seen Agnes the moment they had entered the room—had seen her left eyebrow arch with disapproval the way it so often did. She watched as Agnes quickly studied the man from head to toe, obviously surmising he was nobility, for she pasted on one of her false and wicked smiles as she approached him.

"Good morning, sire," Agnes greeted. "I am Agnes Teche."

"And I am Stavos Voronin," the man began without pause. "My horse nearly trampled this girl in the street only moments ago, and she has sustained injury. I understand she labors under your employ, and I have come to ask that she be given the day to recover from the injuries I have inflicted upon her."

Again Agnes Teche offered a counterfeit smile of sympathy. Yet she was a hard woman—a heartless woman—no matter who addressed her.

"I cannot afford the loss of labor," Agnes explained. "Not one day. I will have to replace her, sire."

The man inhaled a deep breath, exhaling slowly as if struggling for patience. He looked down into Evony's tear-streaked face and asked, "Are you able to stand for a few moments, miss?"

"O-of course, sire," Evony whispered.

Gently the man removed his arms from the crook of her knees, allowing her feet to gently settle to the floor before releasing her altogether.

"I have explained to you, Mrs. Teche, that the girl's injury is no fault of hers, but rather mine," he stated, striding closer to Agnes.

"Sire—" Evony began. She could work well enough without her ankle, and she could not afford to lose her position with Agnes.

Panic was welling in her, yet the man raised one hand to indicate she should be silent.

"How much loss will come to you, madame, if this girl is absent for but one day?" he asked the seamstress. "You will keep her wages, no doubt. So what is your loss?" He stepped closer to Agnes, yet Agnes stood firm and unwaveringly careless of Evony's situation. "I have nearly killed this girl, and I mean to make recompense for it by any means necessary," Stavos Voronin continued. "How much do you stand to lose in profit?" Evony watched as the stranger reached into a small pocket in his trousers and produced a gold coin.

"No, sire!" Evony gasped.

Yet the narrowed eyes—the icy stare of warning that Agnes Teche glared at her—silenced her at once.

Without hesitation, Agnes Teche reached out, plucking the gold coin from the man's fingers. "One day," she mumbled. "She may have today to rest her injury. But if she does not return tomorrow…"

Retrieving another gold coin from his pocket, the man offered it to Agnes. "Three days she will rest it, and you will hold her position for her…else I will not be so obliging when next I step into your shop, madame."

Again Agnes did not pause to snatch the coin the man offered. "Agreed," she said.

Near instantly, Evony found herself swept up into the man's arms once more. She was astonished into silence—that the man would offer Agnes Teche more than a fortnight's profit in return for three days to allow Evony to recover. She could not conceive it at first.

As the man, Stavos, began to stride from the room to exit the shop, he paused. Turning toward Agnes Teche once more, he commented, "I understand you were one of the queen's favored seamstresses."

Agnes Teche smiled with pride, straightened her posture, tipped her nose higher into the air, and said, "Yes, sire. I was."

"Then your seamstressing must be far more favorable than either your countenance or moral character. Good day, Mrs. Teche," Stavos Voronin said.

As Evony's mouth hung agape with astonishment, the man strode over the shop's threshold and into the street once more.

"How do you tolerate that old crone?" he grumbled, scowling as the intensity of his blue eyes captured the as yet astonished green of her own.

"Sire, you just gave Agnes Teche more wages than she earns in a fortnight," Lovie explained, "and you presented offense as you retreated."

"I know her breed," the man responded. "Coin is the only thing that moves her. Not even criticism will wound her...as long as there is money in her pocket." He glanced down to Evony again, and she was surprised as she felt a blush rise to her cheeks. "So your name is Evony," he stated.

"Yes, sire," Evony affirmed.

"I am Stavos," the man offered. He then looked to Lovie and asked, "And you, milady, are?"

"Lovie Wiggin, sire," Lovie answered, also blushing. "Widowed citizen of Abawyth, friend of Evony...and foe of Agnes Teche."

Stavos smiled at Lovie, amused by her response. "Very well, Lovie Wiggin, foe of Agnes Teche. Where does this injured kitten of yours reside?"

"Kitten?" Evony quietly exclaimed with mild indignation.

But Lovie only laughed as she answered, "This way, sire."

"Bromius! Follow," the man commanded. Again the enormous gelding snorted and then followed his master through the streets of Abawyth.

"This is where Evony and her young siblings reside," Lovie explained as she gestured toward the door leading to the hovel Evony shared with Mikol and Tressa. "I live in the rooms just next to these," Lovie continued.

"Sire...please put me down," Evony pleaded. "My brother and sister are not used to strangers entering our home. I wouldn't want them to—"

"Ah, but they know me as well as if I were their grandmother," Lovie interrupted. "I'll go in first."

Again Evony felt herself blushing—this time with humiliation—and she was disappointed with herself for such feelings. The rooms in which she, Mikol, and Tressa hid and resided were warm and comfortable for the most part, and she was grateful for them. Yet something in her did not want this Stavos to see how humbly they existed. He was obviously a very wealthy man, and she knew he was not used to such dismal circumstances. Furthermore, she knew he would think she and her family were far beneath him—and what he thought of them concerned her more than she wanted to admit to herself.

"Darlings!" Lovie called as she opened the door before them and stepped into the hovel. "I've brought your sister and a kind man we met in the village just this morning."

"Oh, Lovie!" Tressa exclaimed, leaping from her chair before the hearth and dashing toward the door. "We are so glad you have returned! Mikol and I are near starving to death—I swear it!" Yet the moment Stavos stepped into the room carrying Evony, Tressa gasped. "Evony! What has happened to you? Are you well?"

"I am," Evony assured her little sister.

"Lands! Look at that animal!" Mikol exclaimed then, dashing out the door to better see Bromius. "Is he yours, sire?" he asked, glancing up to Stavos a moment.

"Yes," the man answered, grinning at Mikol's delight.

Mikol shook his head with admiration. "He's a wonderful horse!" he noted. "Look at his stature."

"This is my brother, M-Michael," Evony stammered. "And my sister, Tess."

"I am honored to meet you both," Stavos said, looking first from Mikol and then to Tressa.

"The honor is ours, I assure you, sire," Tressa responded, dropping a polite and very graceful curtsey.

"Certainly," Mikol greeted, offering a hand to Stavos.

Even though the man still cradled Evony in his arms, he managed to awkwardly accepted Mikol's handshake. "That's a firm grip you have, Michael," he chuckled.

"Thank you, sire," Mikol said with a proud nod.

"But what happened to you, Evony?" Tressa asked once more.

"Oh, nothing to speak of," Evony lied. "I was not being careful when crossing the street and Mr. ...Lord...Mr. Stavos's horse startled me. I twisted my ankle a little is all."

"I, however, have robbed your sister of not only a day's wage from that old crone she stitches for," Stavos began, smiling as both Mikol and Tressa giggled at his calling Mrs. Teche a crone, "but also of your breakfast." Striding to one of the chairs sitting before the hearth, Stavos deposited Evony into it and continued. "Therefore, I was wondering if perhaps the two of you, along with your friend Miss Lovie here, might see to your sister's ankle whilst I return to the village to acquire a replacement for the eggs Bromius and I destroyed."

"Of course we will see to her, sire," Mikol assured the man. "But there is no need for you to worry over the eggs. We have plenty." It was an untruth, of course—that they had plenty. Mikol well knew there would be no breakfast for him and Tressa without the eggs. But he was ever the young gentleman.

"Yes, please, sire," Evony interjected. "Please do not heighten the weight of my debt to you. I cannot make recompense as it is, and—"

"You owe me nothing, miss," Stavos interrupted, however. "Your injury and loss of wages—and the loss of your breakfast—they are all my doing, and I will see that I make amends."

"Sire, please," Evony pleaded, new tears filling her eyes. It was so gallant of him to do all he had done—to offer more. But Evony feared his good deeds had already drawn too much attention to her, Mikol, and Tressa. If King Standwood were to hear even Evony's name spoken...

Evony was rendered breathless, however—all thoughts and fears scattered from her mind—as the man suddenly knelt before her, taking her hands in his own.

"I know there is more here than my eyes are seeing, Miss Evony," he said in a lowered voice—a voice that was reassuring and warm, like heated milk and honey just before bed. "And I promise I will speak of none of this…not to anyone. I swear it to you. But I pray you let me remain honorable. Allow me to replace your meal. It is the very least I can offer."

"Please let him bring us the eggs that were broken, Evony," Tressa begged, putting a comforting arm around Evony's shoulders. Then she whispered, "I'm so terribly hungry," into Evony's ear.

More tears welled in Evony's eyes—tears of fatigue, of pain from her injury, and of hunger—tears of defeat for the sake of Mikol and Tressa.

Meeting Stavos's insistent gaze, Evony nodded. "V-very well."

"Thank you," Stavos said, exhaling a heavy sigh. He smiled and asked, "How many eggs were lost?"

"Six," Evony admitted.

Rising to his full, towering height, Stavos smiled. "Then I shall return shortly." He looked to Tressa, saying, "And you shall have your breakfast." Striding toward the door, he paused. Watching Mikol study Bromius a moment, he then said, "Would you be willing to keep him for me while I retrieve the eggs from the village? He's had a long ride and could use some rest."

"Of course, sire! Of course!" Mikol exclaimed with sheer resplendence brightening his countenance. "I'd be very honored."

"Thank you, Michael," Stavos said. "I won't be long."

Mikol nodded.

Stavos chuckled and tousled the boy's dark hair. "May I speak with you a moment, Lovie Wiggin?" Stavos asked Lovie then.

"O-of course, sire. Of course," Lovie agreed.

"Tressa," Evony whispered to her sister, "quickly, go and listen to what the man is saying to Miss Lovie!"

But Tressa gasped with righteous indignation. "Evony! I can't! Eavesdropping? Mother says it's terribly bad manners to eavesdrop!"

"I know, darling…I know," Evony agreed. "But you remember how different things are now? The danger we're all in? I need to know what the man is saying to Miss Lovie about us…if he suspects anything."

"Very well, Evony," Tressa sighed with disappointment. "But please…don't ever tell Mother I've eavesdropped."

Evony forced a smile, simultaneously heartbroken and moved by Tressa's enduring hope where their mother was concerned. "I promise I won't tell anyone…not ever."

With another exhaled sigh of disappointment in herself, Tressa rather trudged toward the front door. Yet the moment she saw Mikol stroking the velvet nose of Bromius, the memory of the task Evony had given her was as fleeting as a snowflake on an ember.

Evony sighed with defeat, though she couldn't help but smile as she watched her brother and sister stroke the magnificent horse—speak to him in the kind, reassuring voices that only children owned.

"Thank you, Lovie Wiggin," Stavos said, pressing a gold coin into the woman's wrinkled palm. "And not a word to your friends, eh?"

Lovie Wiggin nodded. "Not a word, sire." She looked up into Stavos's face then, and he was struck by the deep emotion he saw in her faded blue eyes. "You are very kind, sire…especially for a nobleman."

Stavos chuckled. "Kind? Maybe," he said. "But I have all too many faults and failings, Lovie Wiggin. Let us hope you never discover those, that they cause you to forget my more praiseworthy qualities. Hmmm?"

Lovie Wiggin smiled, nodding at him. She turned then to return to the home of Evony and her siblings. Stavos watched her go a moment. She was a kind woman, and obviously a loyal friend—loyal enough to confess to Stavos that Evony and her young brother and sister were in dire need of food, yet also loyal enough not to reveal too much to him concerning their history, of how they came to be parentless and living in a hovel in the kingdom of Abawyth.

But Stavos Voronin was not as blind-eyed as many nobles and royals. Evony's physical gestures—even the simplest movement of her hands—revealed that she had not always been destitute. The same was true of the children—of their polished manners and the boy's knowledge of horses and tendency to be bold and fearless of strangers.

Ah yes, Stavos enjoyed a good mystery. After all, interest in the inexplicable circumstances surrounding the royals of Abawyth was the very thing that had lured him to the kingdom—the enigma of Abawyth's twelve sleepy princesses. And yet now—now his mind was all the more intrigued. Not only was the obscurity of what had caused the profound and baffling torpidity of Abawyth's princesses laid out before him, but also he found his curiosity intensely piqued over the riddle surrounding the very lovely Evony and her siblings.

Evony herself was quite beautiful—hair the color of roasted chestnuts and eyes that shimmered like polished jade. She was thin and weary—obviously from lack of nourishment and from miserable labor under the seamstress's crow-like eyes. But her beauty and grace were fully evident still, no matter how she had tried to hide them under tattered clothing. No—Evony had not always labored hard at stitching for the old crone Agnes Teche.

As he strode toward the butcher's shop, Stavos's mind began to concoct scenarios of her possible history. Was she the daughter of a once-wealthy lord who had squandered his riches on women and wine and then died to leave his children in poverty? Were she, her brother, and her sister in truth this Lovie Wiggins's illegitimate grandchildren, born of some nobleman's immoral escapade with a chambermaid yet raised by governesses who taught them the ways of nobles?

As Stavos strode through the village resting on the outskirts of Abawyth Castle, his mind reeled with possibilities. In fact, so overtaken was he with thoughts of this Evony and her young siblings that it was not until he entered the butcher's shop in search of a ham for their breakfast and heard the patrons speaking of the young lord of Pariveth being dismissed by the king early that morning that his musings were drawn back to why he had come to Abawyth at all—to solve the conundrum surrounding the twelve beautiful princesses of Abawyth kingdom—to solve the seemingly impenetrable crux and thereby win the hand of one of Abawyth's princesses, as his father, King Letholdus of Ethiarien, had commanded.

My everlasting admiration, gratitude, and love.
To my husband, Kevin,
My inspiration,
My heart's desire…
The man of my every dream!

ABOUT THE AUTHOR

Marcia Lynn McClure's intoxicating succession of novels, novellas, and e-books—including *The Visions of Ransom Lake*, *A Crimson Frost*, *Dusty Britches*, and most recently *The Secret Bliss of Calliope Ipswich*—has established her as one of the most favored and engaging authors of true romance. Her unprecedented forte in weaving captivating stories of western, medieval, regency, and contemporary amour void of brusque intimacy has earned her the title "The Queen of Kissing."

Marcia, who was born in Albuquerque, New Mexico, has spent her life intrigued with people, history, love, and romance. A wife, mother, grandmother, family historian, poet, and author, Marcia Lynn McClure spins her tales of splendor for the sake of offering respite through the beauty, mirth, and delight of a worthwhile and wonderful story.

BIBLIOGRAPHY

A Bargained-For Bride
Beneath the Honeysuckle Vine
A Better Reason to Fall in Love
The Bewitching of Amoretta Ipswich
Born for Thorton's Sake
The Chimney Sweep Charm
Christmas Kisses-Three Favorite Holiday Romances
A Crimson Frost
Daydreams
Desert Fire
Divine Deception
Dusty Britches
The Fragrance of her Name
A Good-Lookin' Man
The Haunting of Autumn Lake
The Heavenly Surrender
The Highwayman of Tanglewood
Kiss in the Dark
Kissing Cousins
The Light of the Lovers' Moon
Love Me
The Man of Her Dreams
The McCall Trilogy
Midnight Masquerade
An Old-Fashioned Romance
One Classic Latin Lover, Please
The Pirate Ruse
The Prairie Prince
The Rogue Knight
Romantic Vignettes-The Anthology of Premiere Novellas
Saphyre Snow
Shackles of Honor
The Secret Bliss of Calliope Ipswich